PRAISE FOR

"Rick Skwiot proves himself   deftly
knits the threads of this s'   pelling—
and surprising—concl   ucceeds, and
does so with compassio.

    -Michael .   ard-winning author
     of *Fu   e* and *The Flinch Factor*

"Hardboiled and hard-hitting, Skwiot's *Fail* delivers a grit-
ty knockout crime story you won't soon forget."
    -Brian Wiprud, author of *The Clause*

"Chicago has Scott Turow, Boston Dennis Lehane, LA
James Elroy. Finally St. Louis has its laureate of fiction, Rick
Skwiot. His new novel, *Fail*, is a sheer success. Skwiot hits
for the fences and stylishly touches all the bases—money,
municipal politics, police corruption, infidelity, suicide,
homicide, all rendered in crackling prose."
    -Michael Mewshaw, author of *Sympathy for the Devil:*
    Four Decades of Friendship with Gore Vidal

"*Fail* is a riveting spellbinding tale with intricate characters
that are depicted through carefully crafted imagery of iconic
St. Louis landmarks bolstered by lucid vernacular accuracy
reflecting the rich cultural diversity of the city."
    -John Baugh, author of *Beyond Ebonics:*
    Linguistic Pride and Racial Prejudice and
    former director African and African American
    Studies, Washington University in St. Louis

Other books by Rick Skwiot

Death in Mexico
Sleeping With Pancho Villa
Key West Story
Christmas at Long Lake: A Childhood Memory
San Miguel de Allende, Mexico: Memoir of a
Sensual Quest for Spiritual Healing

FAIL

a novel

RICK SKWIOT

Blank Slate Press | Saint Louis, MO 63110

Cover design by Kristina Blank Makansi
Cover image: drolet /iStock

Library of Congress Control Number: 2014948219
ISBN: 9780985808686

In memory of my father,
Edward Joseph Skwiot

FAIL

RICK SKWIOT

Every time you stop a school,
you will have to build a jail.

- Mark Twain

- | -

Alonzo Watkins got shot thanks to Christmas. The university library, where he had been cocooning most evenings for the past four months, closed early that Friday for Christmas break. So he took the 9:35 bus home instead of the 11:35. Bad timing.

The number 4 Natural Bridge in which he was riding slid to a stop. Alonzo looked up from the chess game on his iPad and saw the driver staring at him in the rearview mirror.

"You said 'Salisbury Street,' right?"

He glanced out into the dark, recognized where they were, and rose, shoving the computer into his backpack as he moved toward the front door. It opened with a hiss.

"Thank you, ma'am."

"You take care, son. And merry Christmas."

He stepped down into fresh snow, which came to the top of his beige chukkas. The bus, its yellow-lit interior now empty of passengers, lumbered ahead, turning south on Parnell Street to head downtown. Alonzo slipped the backpack over his shoulder, pulled his stocking cap down on his head, and marched east on Salisbury.

He had the northwest wind at this back, but snow

swirled between the redbrick tenements, down the redbrick alleys, and across brick-strewn vacant lots, biting his face. His legs, protected from the Arctic chill by only his jeans, stung from the cold. Four blocks until he reached home on Hyde Park. He hoped his sister's kids would be asleep but feared they'd still be watching TV.

The snow flew past yellow streetlights. A few homes were lit. In one first-story window a Christmas tree with multi-colored lights sat behind iron bars. Others, with windows boarded, loomed cold, dark, lifeless, and ghostly.

On the next corner he saw the broad windows of the confectionary—usually dimmed by the time he passed—still aglow behind their crisscrossed steel grill. Alonzo dug his bare hands deep into the pockets of his wool jacket and kept trudging ahead.

When he noticed three hooded figures emerge from the store he crossed to the sidewalk on the far side of the street, keeping his eyes on the white ground in front of him. Like always, Alonzo tried to disappear, strove to become invisible. But on the periphery he saw the trio cross the deserted street and fall in behind him. He quickened his pace.

"The fuck you think you're going, college boy?"

Alonzo kept walking, heart speeding.

"A yo. I'm talking to you, pussy!"

"What's in the bag, homeboy?" came a second voice.

He felt a tug on his backpack and whirled.

Despite their hoodies and the snow blowing in his eyes he recognized the middle one, Marlon. They'd been freshmen together at Beaumont High four years earlier. But then Marlon had stopped going.

"I got nothing for you." Alonzo's voice cracked as he said it.

"See about that," said the fat one on the left, grabbing the backpack.

Alonzo yanked on it, ears burning hot, adrenaline fueling him. Fatso jerked it toward him; Alonzo pulled against him. The zipper split open, notebooks, grammar book, chess clock, and iPad tumbling out into the snow.

Marlon stooped to snatch the computer. Alonzo dove forward to wrench it from his grasp. Someone booted him in the head.

Sprawled on the snowy sidewalk, he took another kick, this one in the ribs. Had he the time and the wherewithal to think about it dispassionately, Alonzo likely would have taken his beating, relinquished his iPad, and slunk off. Instead, however, the instincts of a cornered animal rose within him.

Somehow he got to his knees and began flailing with his fists. A wild right caught Marlon, who dropped the iPad and brought his hands to his nose, from which blood began to spurt. He straightened, jammed his right hand into his pocket, and withdrew a small caliber automatic.

Panting, Alonzo froze and fixed on the gun's barrel gleaming golden in the streetlight, vibrating. Marlon, wide-eyed, speechless, stood over him, shaking.

"Do the motherfucker, Marlon! Nigga busted your damn nose! Do him!"

Alonzo scrambled to his feet, turned and ran across the street toward Hyde Park, his breath coming in short bursts, chest heaving. Then he felt a bee sting in his back and heard the dull explosion of the gun, muffled by the snow.

He wheezed, trying to catch his breath. His legs buckled beneath him, dropping him once again to his knees. The sting in his back grew hot and spread, radiating throughout his chest. He fell forward, the snow cooling his face. Now the cold felt good, and he sensed himself slipping off somewhere strange and soothing....

- 2 -

Carlo Gabriel sat with his topcoat in his lap studying the mayor's portrait on the wall across the room. Despite the high ceilings and the cold outside, the inside air hung warm. Memories hung in the air as well, which he kept brushing back.

Without apparent cue, the bow-tied man behind the desk said, "Ms. Cantrell will see you now."

Gabriel lifted himself and sauntered toward the tall door ahead, which now swung open. A statuesque brunette in a business suit appeared and shook his hand.

"Sorry to keep you waiting, detective. Call from channel five on the snow removal—or lack thereof."

He thought to correct her on the detective title—"That's *Lieutenant* Gabriel, ma'am"—but then thought better of it. Now that he was reduced to doing detective work, that's what he seemed to most people.

He stepped onto a Persian carpet. She closed the door behind him and walked ahead to an oversized walnut desk and high-backed leather chair. The tall windows boasted a view of the cityscape behind her—the Civil Courts Building, the Old Courthouse, the Gateway Arch. Impressive. Her hair was held in place by a bone barrette in back; her suit—

black pinstriped—featured a tight skirt that did not quite reach the backs of her knees. Gabriel pursed his lips. Of course he had seen her on television when she worked as an anchorwoman. But he had never seen her legs.

She indicated a wooden armchair across from her. He sat and laid his topcoat on the chair next to him. When he faced her she took in and let out a breath.

"My husband disappeared three days ago."

He leaned forward. "Three days ... Saturday then."

She nodded. He reached for his coat, black cashmere, and removed a notepad from its pocket. "When did you last see Mr. Cantrell?"

"Stone. Jonathan Stone. He left our apartment Saturday morning. I was still in bed."

Despite the feeble winter sun her skin looked tanned. High cheekbones. Her perfume floated to him. "Where do you live?"

"The ABCs on Kingshighway. We own a condo there."

He knew the building—a very correct address for urban white folks.

"Why did you wait three days before filing a report?"

She lifted a finger to her lips, full and pouting. "Is that what we're doing, filing a report?"

"Just a manner of speaking, Ms. Cantrell. I understand the mayor wants it handled right."

"I want it handled right. No need making anything official until we have to. I pray we won't have to. He could show up anytime."

She meant alive, surely. "So he's been gone overnight previously? Without your knowing about it beforehand, I mean."

"No, never."

"Was he depressed?"

She blinked. "Jonathan wouldn't kill himself, if that's what you're thinking."

"Any drug or alcohol issues? Sorry, I have to ask these questions. No disrespect intended."

"No."

"You've been married how long?"

"Twelve years. We met at Mizzou."

"Children?"

She shook her head.

"He hasn't shown up at work?"

She shook it again. "They're on semester break. He's a college professor."

"In what field?"

"English."

"I presume money's not an issue—gambling losses?"

She sniffed. "Jonathan wouldn't be caught dead in a casino."

"Any personal problems?"

A hesitation then, "You mean does he have a mistress?"

Gabriel shrugged a shoulder. It happens. Even when your wife is fine, and Ellen Cantrell was fine. "Whatever problems."

"Jonathan's a very private person. Keeps things inside."

"Health issues?"

"Even being around students, he never gets sick."

"How old is he?"

"Thirty-four."

Gabriel nodded remembering what it was like at thirty-four. A pivotal age for many men, fueled by a mix of ambition, testosterone, and hope. But for him that was two decades past and he wondered how much he had left.

"What about family members, parents, siblings…?"

"I emailed his mother—they live in Florida now. I was indirect but she obviously knows nothing. He was an only child."

"The last time you saw him was Saturday morning?"

"I didn't actually see him. As I said I was still in bed."

"You share the same bed?"

Cantrell lowered her chin and studied Gabriel's silk scarf, purple, draped down the lapels of his black blazer. It was the sort of question asked of a connected white woman that, in earlier times, could have earned a black cop trouble.

She lifted her eyes to meet his. He stared back, waiting for an answer, but all he got was, "I heard the front door closing."

"What time was this?"

"Around ten."

Gabriel made a note. "Were you up late Friday night?"

"At the mayor's Christmas party. In the ballroom at the Mayfair. It was one o'clock when we left." Gabriel sat still, waiting for more. Eventually she went on. "I was working, not partying. There were media people and others we have special relationships with. I try to make sure there's no miscommunication."

He raised an eyebrow. His Honor, he knew from their days together, liked his gin. Which at times made him shoot from the hip, figuratively speaking.

"And what was your husband doing during this time?"

"Mingling, I guess. People watching."

"Did he get drunk?"

"Not so I noticed."

"Did he drive home?"

"We took a cab. Jonathan had come downtown on the train."

"What did you talk about in the cab?"

"I was talked out. Jonathan was his usual quiet self. When we got to Forest Park it had started snowing. He commented on how pretty it was."

"Do you own a car?"

"Yes, a Jeep. I also have a city vehicle. Jonathan rides the MetroLink to campus."

"And the Jeep is gone?"

"It wasn't in the garage when I went down Saturday afternoon."

"When did you first begin to worry?"

"Saturday evening. Not worry so much as wonder. I called his cell phone from a party fundraiser and got no answer. When I got home around midnight I tried again and heard it ring in the den."

"Does he usually carry it?"

"Not always. He's a reader not a talker."

"Did he leave a note or mention a trip?"

"Not that I recall."

"Any friends or colleagues we might check with?"

"Jonathan's always been a loner. There may be colleagues at work, but none that I know. None in whom he would confide."

"Any withdrawals?"

"No."

Gabriel scribbled on his notepad: "Wife checked bank accounts—why?" As he did, he saw her looking at her watch.

"One last question, Ms. Cantrell. Why did you wait three days to involve the police?"

She stood and glared down at him, jaw moving laterally as if grinding teeth. He often got interesting reactions when he asked the same question twice.

"I didn't. Others have been on this since Sunday morning. Checking the accidents, incidents, hospitals."

Who, he wondered? He visualized the chain of command: The mayor, Chief of Police Donnewald, Bureau Commander Coleman, Deputy Commander Masters, Fourth District Captain Stolle.... But the usual chain of command didn't apply here; otherwise he wouldn't be having this conversation.

Gabriel flipped closed his notepad, pushed himself up from the armchair with a sigh, and handed her his card.

"I'd appreciate it if you could email me a recent photo of your husband. I'll keep you posted on any developments."

She studied the card and slipped it into her pocket. "You understand, lieutenant, that everything comes through me first," she said, walking around the desk. "Clear?"

Her long legs were nothing like those of his ex-wife, Janet, but her mouth was.

"Yes, ma'am, I understand. The mayor underscored that."

Outside her office, he let out a breath. He moved back down City Hall's grand staircase to the ground floor and crossed the lobby, heels clicking on the white marble.

"Brother Gabriel!"

He stopped and turned. An old black man in a baggy gray suit, carrying a Bible, approached. They slapped hands.

"Preacher Cairns! Thought you'd be in heaven by now. How's biz?"

"Slow, slow. No one thinks to get married when it snows. You back downtown?"

"Not yet. Still in exile. Just checking my traps."

The old man laughed then sobered. "It ain't the same these days."

"Nope," Gabriel said. "Not even close."

§

From downtown Gabriel drove his unmarked Dodge north on the interstate. Minimal traffic. He tracked a snowplow shooting salt out its tail. At the university he exited and followed signs to Rysman Hall. Before its doors he stomped snow from his black Ferragamos and stepped inside the tall brown-brick building. He rode the elevator to the fifth floor and wandered down a narrow hallway of closed office doors until he found room 544. He knocked.

"Enter!"

He pushed the door open and stuck his head through. An ebony man two shades darker than Gabriel with shaved head sat half-hidden behind books and papers stacked on a metal desk.

"Professor Betancourt?" The man looked up from a document, reading glasses on his nose. "I'm Lieutenant Gabriel."

The man rose and extended a hand. Betancourt came up to Gabriel's chin. He wore faded designer jeans and a black merino sweater. His eyes lively and penetrating. They shook hands—manicured nails, like his own.

Betancourt moved a stack of papers from a chair and nodded at it. "Excuse the mess. It's never tidy but particularly chaotic at semester's end."

"No semester break for you?"

"A department chair is a two-headed monster—half faculty, half administration—and both eat hours."

"This shouldn't take long."

Both men sat. Gabriel let his eyes roam over the bookshelves that ran floor to ceiling along the north wall: a jumble of hardbacks and paperbacks with stapled documents stuffed in between. English literature—he recognized Hardy, Austen, Dickens—and literary criticism, about which he knew nothing. Behind Betancourt a window afforded a view of a gray sky and a parking garage whose top floor had not been plowed.

"On the phone you said it was a confidential matter."

Gabriel showed him his police I.D. and gold-plated badge. "I'd appreciate it if we could keep our conversation just between the two of us for now. It may turn out to be nothing."

"I hope a student isn't in trouble."

"It seems that one of your faculty members hasn't been seen for a few days and his wife is worried. We're looking into it, but it's likely nothing."

"Who is it?"

"Professor Stone."

Betancourt lifted his chin. "*Adjunct* Professor Stone."

"Adjunct?"

Betancourt smiled as if a student had given him the wrong answer. "An adjunct is not a regular faculty member but a part-time instructor. Jonathan Stone taught three sections of composition and a class in remedial grammar."

"Sounds like full-time."

Betancourt shook his head. "No committee responsibilities, no benefits."

"And the pay?"

He shrugged. "I don't know what we're paying adjuncts now. There's a standard rate depending on degree status. Stone, I believe, was ABD." Gabriel frowned. "All But Dissertation," Betancourt explained. "An MA who has done the PhD coursework but has not yet completed his dissertation."

"Do you know Stone well?"

"Hardly at all. He was hired by my predecessor. We may have spoken only a handful of times." Betancourt picked up a pen and began tapping it on his desk pad.

Gabriel asked: "Do you know if he had any friends in the department who might be able to help me?"

"No idea. Perhaps his office mate."

"May I see Professor Stone's office?"

Betancourt stopped tapping the pen. "Stone no longer has an office." Gabriel waited. "Adjuncts teach on a semester-by-semester basis."

"He quit?"

"Stone was not invited back."

"Who does the inviting?"

"That would be my decision."

"Any particular reason?"

Perfect silence except for the radiator's white noise, which Gabriel now became aware of. A few snowflakes fell outside.

"University teaching is a highly competitive field. We have other adjuncts and graduate instructors who were performing at a higher level and deserved more hours."

"How long has he taught here?"

"Not sure. He was here when I came five years ago."

Gabriel nodded. Tough getting fired after five, maybe ten years on the job—even if it was a low-paying one.

"When did you inform Professor Stone—*Adjunct* Professor Stone—that he wouldn't be asked back?"

"I didn't speak to him."

"Then how would he have learned that he was being dismissed?"

"Not dismissed. His contract expired. I suspect he may have learned from my secretary."

"Who is?"

"Martha Walczyk."

Gabriel reached into his coat pocket and withdrew his notebook and pen. He scribbled a note—"Betancourt prick. Secretary Martha Walczyk"—and returned them to his pocket.

"She in today?"

Betancourt stood and managed a smile. "Rain or shine, sleet or snow."

In the copy room at the Xerox machine, Gabriel found a fifty-year-old woman in a red dress with a glittery snowman brooch pinned above her heart.

"I'll bet you're Ms. Walczyk."

"*Mrs.* Walczyk."

Gabriel sighed. "All the good ones get married young."

She smiled, retrieved a stack of documents from the machine and led him from the room. "You must want something badly and quickly. Are you from Administration?"

"In a way." He showed her his badge as she sat behind her desk in a windowless room. "Dr. Betancourt said you might be able to help me."

Her smile disappeared. "I hope there's no trouble."

"Probably isn't. Just doing a background check on one of your faculty members, Jonathan Stone."

"What for?"

"We're just trying to track him down."

She brought her hand to her mouth. "Oh, dear. He's disappeared?"

Gabriel thought she might cry. He said, "Look. Between us it's just that he hasn't been home for a few days and his wife is worried."

She began to nod and flicked her eyes in the direction of Betancourt's office. "He came in Friday to say goodbye."

"How did he seem?"

"Pleasant, as always, as least with me. But you never know with him. Still waters run deep. I heard …." She leaned forward, elbows on the desktop. "I heard that at the faculty gathering he had words with Dr. Betancourt. I'm not sure how it started, but I can guess. I hope he's okay."

"Probably just taking a little vacation. Can I see his office, Mrs. Walczyk?"

"Martha." She lifted a glass plate from the corner of her desk. "Christmas cookie?"

Gabriel patted his paunch while studying them. "Maybe just one…."

She led him to Stone's office and unlocked the door. Two desks facing either wall. A narrow window overlooking the road below. Stone's desk held little of interest: pens, paperclips, textbooks on expository writing and grammar. Empty files.

Conversely, the other desk held a stack of blue exam

booklets beneath a yellow rubber-duck paperweight, three coffee mugs with photos of African American children imprinted, and two shelves of American literature: Mark Twain, Henry James, Walt Whitman; Ellison, Morrison, Wright; Thoreau, Cather, Hemingway, Faulkner. On the wall beside the desk hung a framed poster of small white seals on a flashing rainbow-ed disco floor. "Stop clubbing, baby seals!" read the headline, and underneath that, "Punctuation Rules!" Another poster said: "The past, present, and future walk into a bar. It was tense." English-professor humor differed from cop humor.

"Who sits there, Martha?"

"Dadisi."

"Dadisi who?"

"Just plain Dadisi."

"Male, female?"

"Oh, he's a guy." She indicated a yellowed photo on his desk of a youthful black man in a dashiki and Afro with a young woman who held twin boys on her lap.

"He from Africa?"

"East St. Louis."

Gabriel raised his eyebrows. "Still lives there?"

She looked at him, nodding. "Even with a family."

He gazed again at the poster of the disco-dancing seals. "Odd sense of humor."

§

He returned on Interstate 70, cordoned by a levee of dirty snow along either side that matched the gray sky. Traffic still thin. Snow day for many though the schools were already on break. Ugly. The old north St. Louis suburbs held rows of post-war bungalows now fallen into disrepair. Some had been bulldozed. The snow helped cover some of the wounds but it was still butt ugly.

He exited at Union Boulevard. No prettier here—a rust-belt industrial neighborhood now largely abandoned. The old Chevy plant. A metal works. Crumbling warehouses. Soon he approached a new one-story concrete bunker where a painted sign hung on the concrete-and-redbrick façade: "North Patrol Division, Home of the 'Real Police'." He always wondered whether that was a swipe at downtown, the Highway Patrol, or the coppers on TV. But they did cover a tough territory—the 6th, 7th, and 8th districts, the city's continually deteriorating North Side.

Another sign in the snow-covered, semi-circular front yard had the same edgy tone: "KEEP OFF THE GRASS." No please, no thank you, just keep off the fucking grass. Nonetheless beneath the snow the public had worn a dirt path through the turf just feet from the sidewalk. He parked the Dodge in the back lot.

Once inside he lifted his chin toward the young officer lurking near the front desk, where bulletproof glass protected the police from any citizens who might wander in through the front door. Beyond the glass, in the lobby, sat vending machines and an ATM—one of the few safe venues on the North Side for fast cash.

"Hey, Bosco! How are those babies doing?"

The Bosnian smiled. "Babies? Mato's in first grade at St. Aloisus."

"Already? Tempus fidgets, my friend. Is The Gecko around?"

"Working from home till his street gets plowed."

At his desk—he'd been given his own glass-encased office in deference to his rank and former status—Gabriel found an email from Ellen Cantrell, a studio photo of her husband attached. Handsome guy: blond, clean-shaven, wire-rimmed glasses, gaunt. Innocent looking. Nice tie. He forwarded it on to The Gecko:

Geeko Gecko—

If you would get off the young wife for a minute to attend to some high-priority official biz much appreciated. Missing person pic attached Jonathan Stone. Adjunct English prof, hubby of mayor's press secretary Ellen Cantrell. Last seen Sat. a.m. Took own Jeep. Check for it and usual credit cards, plane tix, TSA, hospitals, bank accounts, DWI, blotter, etc. No need to involve the Cyber Crimes Unit on this just yet. Shhhh! Also, find me a list of who was working the mayor's party last Friday night.

Next he went to the English Department on the university website. There he found the same color photo Ellen Cantrell had sent him and a brief bio:

Jonathan Stone teaches a variety of undergraduate writing courses, ranging from creative writing to professional writing to composition. His interests in writing and writing pedagogy encompass the use of technology in human communication and learning processes as well as face-to-face and online classroom instruction. His forthcoming PhD dissertation, "The

Masks of Mark Twain," examines the iconic author's use of misidentification, subterfuge, and disappearance in *Adventures of Huckleberry Finn, Pudd'nhead Wilson, A Connecticut Yankee in King Arthur's Court, The Prince and the Pauper*, and other pivotal works.

"What the hell?" Gabriel said aloud.

He sent an email to Stone's university address telling him "There's a police search under way for you. Please let us know if you're okay. Your wife's worried." But he sensed it wouldn't be that easy.

§

At the Downtown YMCA, Gabriel barreled down the lane, sending an opponent tumbling backward to the ancient wooden floor and banking the ball in off the backboard.

"Game!"

"Charging!"

"Bullshit!" barked Gabriel. "You were moving with me."

"You threw an elbow," yelled Fearn as he picked himself up. "You could hurt somebody, you fat ass."

Gabriel gave him a hand up. "If you're so scared, call 911."

"Honor the call, Carlo."

"Alright, pussy, take the ball. But when the big Mexican comes, you better step aside."

"More like an African elephant."

"Halfrican," Gabriel corrected him. "But let's stop the jiving about my weight and ethnicity and play ball."

Fearn's team brought the ball down court but their shot

hit the rim. Gabriel pushed in for the rebound and hit the guard on the fast break for an easy lay-up and the win.

"Inevitable," Gabriel said as the players slapped hands all around, "bad calls notwithstanding. Just a matter of time."

Fearn came and put a hand on his shoulder. "Your time's running out old man. Enjoy it while you can."

"Oh, I am, I am."

Gabriel joined Fearn and two white cops—Mueller and McDiarmid—in the steam room and lowered himself onto the tiles with a sigh as steam billowed about him. He had been coming to the Y since he was a kid. Back then the ten-story brown-brick building, pushing a hundred, had six floors of dormitories, barbershop, tailor shop, and cafeteria, all catering to men only. Though now co-ed and rehabbed over the years, it still felt like a homey, fading men's club.

"I saw Boscovic at the desk this morning. What gives?"

"Didn't you hear?" asked Fearn. "Returned fire and winged some punk in the calf. He's off the streets while IAD screws with it, but it looks good."

Gabriel coughed as he took in the damp air. "I prefer the saturation method—keep shooting till it stops moving. But if Bosco grazed someone in the leg, he meant to graze someone in the leg."

"You like him."

"I like tough cops."

"He tougher than Mad Angelo?" came a voice out of the mist—Mueller.

That was a good question for Gabriel, given his history with the mayor—Mad Angelo Cira—when they were young cops together, and the mayor's feisty reputation, always vaunted at election time. He chose not to answer it directly.

"I wouldn't mess with Bosco. Known him since he was at Vashon and got in trouble."

"Bosco went to high school at Vashon?"

"Balkan War refugee. Hardly spoke a word of English. One of the homeboys came on to his sister in a disrespectful way. Bosco objects and homie pulls a knife. Next thing he knows, Bosco has him facedown on the ground with the knife blade an inch up his ass or thereabouts."

"You'd never guess by looking at him."

"While his fellow Vashon Wolverines were hanging on the corner playing grab-ass, Bosco was killing Serbs. His sister was the only family he had left. Worked with me briefly as a rookie. I remember chasing a perp—some nickel-ass dealer—down an alley where the guy tries to hide under a panel truck. Bosco didn't want to dirty his new uniform wrestling the guy out, so he starts letting the air out of the tires. Dealer exited like he was shot from a cannon."

Mueller and McDiarmid left laughing. When the door closed Fearn said:

"I hear you're on special assignment too."

"Hard to keep secrets."

"Particularly when an exiled lieutenant has a City Hall sit-down with the mayor first thing in the morning."

"Just a little security work, dawg. Part of my rehabilitation."

"Good luck with that. You can have headquarters."

"I will, my man. Gabriel's coming back from Siberia."

- 3 -

The Mississippi had always intrigued Gabriel, ever since he was a kid. Just blocks from the near-North Side neighborhood where he grew up, it had marked the end of his known world, luring him and his pals, who scoured its banks for treasure, played at river pirates, and watched the barges and riverboats ply its swirling brown waters. As teenagers they expanded their horizons, driving across it via the Eads Bridge to East St. Louis for liquor, jazz, and women. Now he used the new bridge to transcend the ice-chunked channel, heading once again to East St. Louis, Illinois, a city that for him had long ago lost its dark allure.

The streets there hadn't seen a snowplow, so Gabriel followed scant tracks left by other vehicles. Not much got done here, not much good. It had the highest crime rate in America. One of every thousand citizens was murdered each year. Yet another city official had recently been arrested for soliciting kickbacks. A newspaper investigation found that one out of four cops had a rap sheet.

He found Dadisi's place—a newer two-story frame town-home on a cul-de-sac amid an urban prairie where redbrick factories and warehouses once stood. Bars covered the windows and front door; the sidewalk and driveway had been shoveled. Snowflakes swirled about as Gabriel made his way from his sedan.

A girl of six or seven cracked the door, stared, and ran off. Dadisi appeared—receding gray Afro now, reading glasses, cable sweater. Gabriel held up his badge and I.D.

Inside, two girls squabbled over schoolwork on a dining-room table to the right. Dadisi took Gabriel's overcoat and brought two coffee cups on saucers to the living room, which smelled of resin from a lit Christmas tree. As the men sat before a gas-log fire, Dadisi turned to the girls and called:

"Take your books up to your room. We've got talking to do."

The girls left without complaint.

"Grandkids?"

Dadisi rolled his eyes. "Afraid not. Wife number two demanded parity with wife number one."

Gabriel studied framed posters from Kenya and Botswana on the walls, hand-carved giraffes and elephants on the coffee table. "Very African of you."

Dadisi smiled. "Very East Side." Then serious: "What's with Stone? You said you had questions."

"This is a confidential inquiry for now. Nothing official."

"I understand."

"You know who his wife is. Well, she hasn't seen him for a few days and the mayor asked me to look into it."

Dadisi studied Gabriel, chewing his lip. "I don't know him that well socially, just professionally. We had lunch on occasion but just talked shop."

"Good enough. What do you know?"

He shrugged. "I know he worked his ass off and still lost

his job. Hell, man, he was teaching four sections of writing classes. And for adjunct pay."

"Which is?"

"Not even three grand per section."

Gabriel looked to the fireplace and African posters. "You too?"

"No, I'm a full-time instructor. American lit. But what Stone taught—composition mainly—is a grind. Twenty students per section, three or four research papers per student, three or four drafts of each that you have to read. Stone couldn't find time to work on his dissertation. That's why he started teaching remedial grammar—just so he wouldn't have so damn many papers to grade."

"Remedial grammar?"

"You go to school?"

"Back in the day. Saint Louis U."

Dadisi shook a finger at Gabriel. "That's why your name's familiar: You played for the Billikens."

"Thirty years and thirty pounds ago."

"I hear you…. Well, we ain't a private Catholic school. And times have changed. We get inner city high school grads and junior college transfers who we have to stick in remedial courses. Stone thought teaching grammar would be easy—shorter papers to grade. You're dealing with writing a good sentence and maybe a logical paragraph instead of essays."

"You saying it wasn't easy for him?"

"It really messed with him. He had no idea—real suburban white bread. He went to Mizzou and before that CBC—a prep school boy. Anyway, he came in the second week of classes in shock. He told me he gave them a diagnostic assignment. 'These kids have gone through twelve years of public school,' he said, 'and still can't write a grammatically correct sentence—something you and I could do in first grade.'

"I told him what was happening in the schools—St. Louis, East St. Louis, Kansas City, where kids keep falling further and further behind. Public school issues weren't on his radar, and he couldn't believe it. So he went digging.

"Stone became obsessed with it. The more he uncovered the more he got sucked in. Quit working on his dissertation to research the schools. Not a good career move, I told him. But he wouldn't listen. And there was something more to it, something else eating at him that he kept close to the vest. Never said anything specific, but something was really driving him."

Gabriel sipped at his coffee, thinking.

"Were you at the faculty party last Friday?"

"I wouldn't call coffee and Christmas cookies a party."

"I heard Stone and Betancourt had an altercation."

"Both are too soft-spoken for an 'altercation.' But they had words."

"What about?'

"It was odd. Never heard Jonathan go off like that on anyone. But he'd had a few drinks at lunch. And he was stressed out. Called Betancourt a 'corrupt son of a bitch.'"

"That sounds pretty heated to me. Betancourt says Stone underperformed—that's why he let him go."

Dadisi shifted in his chair. "I know nothing about that."

Gabriel sipped his coffee again and waited. He heard the girls giggling upstairs and sipped some more. Dadisi studied him, looking over his reading glasses. He licked his lips as if about to speak but apparently decided against it.

"What?"

"Like I said, I know nothing. But if you want to get an idea what sort of teacher Stone was, you might check his student evaluations. Talk to Martha Walczyk."

§

Gabriel drove back across the Mississippi. The St. Louis skyline, once dominated by early redbrick "skyscrapers" of twelve stories, now glistened with towering steel and glass buildings against the gray sky. The Gateway Arch shimmered on the riverfront. As traffic slowed, Gabriel telephoned Walczyk.

"My man Dadisi alerted me to the existence of 'student evaluations.' Would there be some for Professor Stone?"

"There should be a set for each class. On the last day, usually, the instructor distributes the forms and leaves the room so students can give an honest anonymous appraisal. A student then collects them and brings them to my office. The instructor gets copies and the originals go in his personnel file."

"I was wondering, Martha, if I might have a look at the most recent batch for Jonathan Stone."

Silence. Ahead on the bridge a car had spun out in the snow and sat sideways, blocking two lanes. Gabriel slowed. Finally Walczyk said:

"I'd like to help you, lieutenant, but personnel files are confidential. I could not give you access on my own authority. However, if some higher authority issued instructions...."

She paused. Gabriel steered past the stalled car.

"Mrs. Walczyk, as a law enforcement officer serving the citizens of St. Louis, I order you to allow me access to those files as they are vital to my investigation. I take full responsibility."

"Since you put it that way, I'll have copies in this afternoon's mail. You should get them by Thursday."

"Thursday?"

"No mail delivery Wednesday."

"Why not?"

"Christmas."

"Right, right. Let's do this instead: I'll send a cab for them tomorrow morning."

Gabriel hung up and sped away. Christmas. That would throw a wrench into things.

- 4 -

Next morning Gabriel left his apartment on the west side of Forest Park and drove up Union Boulevard to the North Patrol Division. Union used to be a nice street, a major north-south corridor with venerable homes, schools, and businesses. Now it was down-at-the-heels and turning tawdry, and, except for the occasional gas station, the Division office—unornamented, sterile, and institutional— was the only new structure for blocks.

He hated the neighborhood where he was officed, the darkened factories, the nearby pawnshops and check cashing stores. The failure it all signaled. Unkempt yards in the summer with men drinking in vacant lots, many of them obviously under age. Even in wintertime, he'd see them gathered round a fire in a metal drum, passing a bottle. The jobs had gone, but the people remained. Things had deteriorated dramatically since he was a kid, but he didn't know who to blame. Everyone seemed to be doing their job.

He found The Gecko sitting in his cubicle. He even looked like a gecko: slender, chinless, bug-eyed. Nonetheless, The Gecko liked the handle the street cops laid on him. It made him feel like one of the guys.

"Anything on Stone?"

The Gecko perused an oversized computer monitor on the desk in front of him. "Negative, negative, negative, lieutenant. No tickee, no washee, no nothing. No credit card purchases or ATM action. Not arrested, hospitalized, or morgued-up. Did not pass 'Go' at airport security. No bank account or cell-phone activity."

"I could have told you about the latter; he left it at home."

"Interesting."

"You think so?"

"Maybe he was called out suddenly and forgot it in the rush. Or maybe he didn't want to leave a trail."

"Or maybe neither. Stone was a book guy, not a chatterer. Often didn't carry it."

The Gecko swiveled around in his desk chair to face Gabriel. "I note the past tense. You figure he's dead?"

"I figure I'm not the English professor here and don't know dick about verb tenses. Whichever, you better go back and check his previous cell calls. Let's see who he's been talking to."

"Gotcha. Nothing yet on the car either. Maybe it's a carjacking and murder."

"When people lose their job on Friday, seldom do they get carjacked on Saturday."

"Interesting."

"Yeah, that bit is, Gecko. But stick to your computers. You're not ready for detective work. Takes imagination."

"Speaking of computers, what about Stone's?"

"On my way downtown to pick it up from his wife."

The Gecko stared at Gabriel. "Ellen Cantrell, Eyewitness News. I always wanted to screw her—before I was married. Those lips...."

Gabriel patted his shoulder. "Now that shows some imagination, Geck. Maybe there's hope for you after all."

§

Gabriel drove downtown, parked across the street from Police Headquarters, and walked around the corner to City Hall, facing a north wind sluicing cold air down Tucker Boulevard. He mounted the stone steps and ducked inside the building. Used to be anyone could enter City Hall through most any door without a problem. Now the only public entrance was on the east side, where citizens—except for cops—had to surrender their weapons, empty their pockets, and pass through a metal detector. He waved at the officer manning the device and moved around it and up the steps into the rotunda.

The building, modeled after the Parisian city hall and built in 1898, still looked good from the outside, with its ornate towers, pink granite, buff sandstone trim, and burgundy clay-tile roof. Inside, the cavernous rotunda and marble grand staircase were unpeopled. Dim hallways led to gerry-rigged office entrances with cheap paneling and dirty glass. It was depressing.

Ellen Cantrell made him wait fifteen minutes. Finally her secretary—red and green polka-dotted bowtie today— told him to go in.

She sat at her desk, dressed in black—mourning? An odd choice for Christmas Eve. Even he had felt festive enough to don a red silk tie that morning. She did not invite him to sit, instead nodding toward a black-fiber computer bag on the corner of her desk.

"There's his laptop, lieutenant, but I doubt you'll find anything helpful."

Meaning that she had already gone in and checked. Maybe she deleted embarrassing files or photos. Or added some.

"Not much to report yet, Ms. Cantrell. No sign of him. Hasn't used a credit card."

That made her thoughtful. "What else are you doing?"

"We've issued a bulletin on the car but no sign yet. And I'm interviewing co-workers. Nothing from the TSA or elsewhere."

"Is that all? We need to find him."

He noted the use of the plural "we." Maybe that included the mayor. Perhaps others. Now that Gabriel was trucking in the world of literature, language, and grammar, its importance seemed to resonate everywhere.

"I understand your concern. The easiest thing would be to alert the media and have them run a photo."

"I realize it hamstrings you, but this investigation must be discreet. The last thing we want is publicity."

Gabriel puzzled over her aversion to publicity. Seemed like just the thing to speed the case along. Apparently that puzzlement showed, for she went on.

"Of course I'm deeply concerned about Jonathan. But I don't want this to somehow become an embarrassment to the mayor—given my proximity and public presence—if there's nothing to it. I strongly suspect that Jonathan is just off doing research or taking a vacation and forgot to tell me or told me when I was preoccupied."

"A vacation?"

"He's been terribly overworked. Grading papers constantly and writing his dissertation whenever he has a free moment. He's devoted to his students and his profession."

"Did you know, Ms. Cantrell, that he lost his job?"

Two vertical creases formed at the center of her forehead. "You mean he was fired?"

"It comes to that. Not hired back for the new semester. Performance not up to snuff says his department chair."

"That doesn't sound like Jonathan.... Maybe he was consumed by his research."

"Maybe," said Gabriel, reaching for the laptop.

He started to turn away then turned back.

"One last thing, Ms. Cantrell. Do you keep a gun at home?"

"Why?"

"Just trying to rule out things."

"I do. Not Jonathan."

"Have you checked to see if it's still there?"

"It's where it always is, in my purse."

"Really?"

"It's okay, lieutenant. I have a concealed-carry permit. As a reporter I was coming and going at odd hours in odd places. Still do. You know the city."

"Yeah, I know it." Gabriel said.

Outside Cantrell's office a black-haired woman who sat waiting looked up at Gabriel. "Hey there, tall, dark, and handsome."

"I'll cop to tall and dark."

"So they've even got you carrying a computer these days?"

He looked at the satchel in his hand. "No, this is for my virtual lunch—only way I can lose weight."

The woman, Laura Berkman, stood, and Gabriel bent to her as they feigned an embrace. The same perfume, even though that was ancient history.

"Still ferreting out corruption and double-dealing?" he asked.

"A never-ending quest. But it beats the hell out of the copy desk. You back downtown?"

"Off the record? The bureaucracy moves in mysterious ways, but I'm working on it."

She lifted her own computer bag from the floor beside her chair and made toward Ellen Cantrell's office. "Tell me about it over a drink this afternoon. Missouri Grille at four. Some of the old crew are getting together."

"Screw the old crew, for all the good they did me. But 'yes' to the drink. See you then, babe."

He didn't have to think twice about it. He had nothing else on his platter.

- 5 -

Back at the North Division offices, a large envelope from Martha Walczyk sat on his desk. He dropped off Stone's laptop with The Gecko, telling him to have it dusted for prints before he got to work on it which, Gabriel understood, wouldn't happen till Thursday.

Then he drove back downtown to the YMCA for hoops. Basketball was art, meditation, and dance all rolled into one. A few trips up and down the court, a couple of jump shots, and all his thoughts and cares slid from him like warming snow from a pitched roof.

Afterward, he hung around the locker room for a couple hours—shooting the breeze with Fearn on basketball and the job, meditating in the sauna, getting a massage, and reading magazines in the TV room.

He took a walk downtown. No point in going back to the office. Most everyone would be marking time awaiting the holiday. And being "detached" from the organizational chart meant that he worked with little or no supervision.

Snow—turning progressively darker shades of gray—remained in piles along the curbs. Though still mid-afternoon the sky too darkened. His ears stung from the cold.

At Macy's he looked at the window displays. He recalled a similar snowy afternoon some fifty years earlier, holding his mother's hand, his father at her side, gazing at the toy trains and animated puppets. Even then, at that age, he noted the stares his parents drew—a black man with a light-skinned Latina was a rare sight in a largely segregated city. Now, however, whenever he dated a white woman no one seemed to give a damn, or at least didn't make their feelings known.

It was nearly five when Gabriel walked into the Missouri Bar and Grille, a few blocks down Tucker Boulevard from City Hall. For years a hangout for cops, newspaper people, ballplayers, cabbies, and other night prowlers. Open three-hundred-sixty-five days a year and serving food and drinks till three a.m. The blue neon lights and aligned liquor bottles on the back bar made it feel nice and seedy and old-fashioned. Signed photos of celebrities and athletes adorned the walls. Tonight lots of loud conversation. He found Laura Berkman sitting at the bar and managed to squeeze in next to her.

"Thought you had forgotten about me," she said.

"You're always on my mind. Just didn't want to arrive before you did and have to talk to assholes. You know how I am sometimes—capable of 'brutal force' and 'violating civil rights.'"

"Glad to see you've buried the hatchet."

"I'd like to bury it in that bastard's skull. But that's all in the past, right? Now words are my only weapons. I'm getting into literature and language."

Berkman smiled and combed back her hair with her fingers as if to draw attention to her face—still unlined at forty and attractive in a sultry, gypsy way. Large earrings dangling. A slender neck. "You had a drink yet?" Gabriel shook his head. "Then let's get you started."

He ordered a Bud Light and a shot of Dickel, and Berkman said, "I understand you're on special assignment for the mayor."

"I can neither confirm nor deny that rumor."

"You know everything's always off the record with me, Carlo, until you tell me different."

"Let's just say I've got something going that might bring me back to my rightful place in the pecker order."

She smiled. "True enough, that. But at least nowadays there's some dark meat in the queue."

Gabriel grabbed his whiskey as the bartender slid it to him. He took a sip. "My ticket was punched before the shit hit. Captain, maybe even Deputy Commander. Five years and out with a fat pension, then Mexico, Costa Rica, Panama. Somewhere warm with hot babes."

"Join me in Jerusalem."

"Tempting. But I prefer somewhere they don't speak English so there are fewer misunderstandings. Is that that prick Schaeffer?"

Berkman turned. "Saffer. He's a good newspaperman."

Gabriel straightened. "I take issue with that. When you plaster allegations of police misconduct and excessive force on page one and then, six months later when the officer is cleared, you run two paragraphs about it on page twelve, that doesn't strike me as particularly good journalism."

Berkman raised an eyebrow. "You can snow others, but please spare me the rap. We all know the investigation was a whitewash and that you thumped the perp without cause.

Otherwise you would have been reinstated instead of being detached and sent to the gulag for re-education."

Gabriel shifted his shoulders. "When some no-good mother caps one of my men, that's cause enough for me. Besides, I never laid a hand on him, just 'rang up long distance.'"

"Cute that, the phone book atop his head, the nightstick banging it repeatedly with all your two-hundred-fifty pounds behind it. Couldn't have felt good."

"On the contrary, it felt great!"

"I know you were distraught—"

"No, not distraught. Angered. Irate. Way pissed-off."

"Whatever. But next time remember to disable the cameras first or wear your mask."

Gabriel leaned back. "Who told you about the mask?"

"I hope you're joking."

"You never know with me. I'm capable of most anything."

"I find you most capable, lieutenant."

"Good Scout, I always do my best. Now, if over the next week or two I can prove to the mayor how capable I am—professionally, that is—I'll be back downtown with you and yours in the new year."

"Fast work. Must be something hot."

"And top secret."

"Maybe another boilermaker will loosen your tongue."

"Try all you want."

"I intend to."

- 6 -

From the Missouri Grille, Gabriel motored west to his building at the edge of the city limits, facing Forest Park. There he bid good evening to his doorman and palmed a twenty to him. "Merry Christmas, Carl."

"The same to you, Mr. Gabriel," he said, unlocking the elevator.

Gabriel rode to the twentieth floor and stepped across the carpeted hall to the door of his studio. He opened it, dropped his keys on the table and walked to the windows overlooking Forest Park across the street. In the distance, the Art Museum stood majestic atop its hill, floodlit like a golden palace, and on the horizon, some eight miles distant, the Gateway Arch glowed silver. Below on Skinker Boulevard cars hummed past.

He liked living above it all. Part of it was practical. Here he felt secure—no assholes coming through the window when he was away, no vengeful ex-cons or humiliated husbands knocking on his door. But most of all he liked the view. From this vantage everything looked clean and orderly and peaceful, especially when it snowed. He doffed his blazer, loosened his tie, and plucked his holster from his belt, where he carried his secondary pistol, his "off-duty weapon," a small Smith & Wesson seven-shot instead of the larger, standard-issue Berretta nine millimeter that he kept locked away.

Gabriel got a beer from the fridge and sat on the sofa facing the windows that comprised his east wall. He looked at his watch, reached for his cell phone, and dialed.

He heard four rings, then a click and a recording. When it ended he said, "Timmy, this is your father. Merry Christmas to you and Theresa. I know it's late there but I just got in. I hope the kids are well and that they like their gifts. Call when you can."

He set the phone down and reached for his beer. The phone began to buzz. Gabriel answered: "Hey, my man, how you doing?"

"My man?" came a feminine voice. "You know I'm all woman."

Now he glanced at the caller I.D. "Sorry, Justine. I'd just left a message for my son and thought it was him."

"Disappointed?"

"Not at all. Always glad to hear from you."

"You home? I thought you might like a Christmas gift. Things are a bit slow tonight and I owe you one."

Gabriel stood, walked to the window, and looked out at the snow-shrouded park glistening in the streetlights. He pictured her and his lips curled in a smile.

"I am eager to collect on that debt, Justine. But maybe some other time, baby. I've been out drinking since five and by the time you got here I'd be...."

"I'm downstairs in the lot."

A real slow night. Most of her regulars would be with

their families.

"What the hell," he said. "We'll have a party."

He called down to Carl and told him to send her straight up.

She soon came to his door in rabbit coat, tall boots, and frosty lipstick, glistening black hair perfumed and curled. Once inside she slipped from her coat, revealing a skintight red dress that barely covered her ass. Gabriel brought her a vodka gimlet and joined her on the couch. He saw that she had positioned a small box with Christmas wrap on the coffee table.

"For me?"

"You did me a good turn, Carlo, when other cops would of taken advantage."

"Well, you helped me out before."

"I keep my eyes open. I want to keep them gangstas away from us working girls."

He began unwrapping the package. "You know I can't take bribes."

"This ain't no bribe. Just a little bling for my wavy-haired boy." She ran a hand through his hair, which he brushed straight back.

He opened the box to find a thick gold bracelet. "Very nice. Not hot, I presume. Wouldn't do for a police lieutenant to be in possession of stolen property."

"No way, man. I bought it with a credit card."

"Yours?"

"Make any difference?"

"Not really. Thank you, Justine," he said, leaning to kiss her cheek. "Wish I had something to give you."

She licked her whitened lips. "You do. But first you got

to unwrap your other present," she said, shifting her hips.

He slid the red dress up to her waist. She wore a white garter belt holding up white stockings that framed her raven thighs—that was all.

Gabriel smiled. "Very festive," he said, pulling her to him.

§

It was midnight when Justine left, but Gabriel didn't feel tired. Dressed now in a blue silk robe, he went to the kitchen and poured himself a bourbon on the rocks. On the kitchen table he spied the manila envelope he had carried home with him and took it to the sofa, where Justine's perfume lingered.

He retrieved the remote control from the coffee table. On the TV screen he selected "Traditional Christmas – Instrumental" then found streaming video of a log fire. He recognized the first tune: "O, Little Town of Bethlehem." It made him think of the crèche that his mother arranged beneath their Christmas tree, and of the manger scene in the plaza of her hometown in Jalisco, where he had visited as a teenager. As Christmas day approached, the plaster representations there of the Three Wise Men were moved progressively closer and closer to the Christ child. But sentimental thoughts of his mother pulled him where he didn't want to go. He again grabbed the remote and found some holiday jazz: George Benson, Nina Simone, Wynton Marsalis.

Gabriel sipped at the bourbon then pulled off the packing tape that sealed the thick envelope. From it he slid a stack of documents paper-clipped in four batches. Three of them were from Stone's freshman composition classes, the fourth from his remedial grammar section. He started with the composition evaluations.

The students first rated Stone on a scale of one to five, five being the highest, in seven areas: setting clear objectives, accessibility, preparation, effectiveness, et cetera.

Below that were ten ruled lines for "COMMENTS."

As Gabriel perused the forms, he saw that Stone got twos and threes across the board from most students. That perhaps related to a number of comments on grading, including: "Impossible to get an A. UNFAIR!" and "WTF! I worked my ass off and still got a C."

But there were a few students who apparently appreciated the high academic standards, giving Stone fives in all categories and praising him. They wrote things like: "A really valuable course," and "Stone is a great, passionate teacher. Wasted on the slackers in class."

There were also a couple comments—in feminine handwriting—that dealt with the professor as a man rather than a teacher. One read, "Stone is hot! I could eat him up." Another student wrote, "I'd love to be home-schooled by Mr. Stone," and included a phone number.

Gabriel stroked his narrow mustache. But the bottom line was that Stone was a demanding, knowledgeable, and helpful instructor for those students keen to learn. For those looking for an easy grade and just going through the motions, he was The Professor from Hell.

Gabriel moved on to the remedial grammar stack. Here the evaluations were also inconsistent but with one striking difference. The remedial grammar students—those who came in unable to compose a grammatically correct sentence—wrote extended comments that often continued on the back of the evaluation form and contained numerous corrections and spelling changes in the writer's own hand:

> "On the first day he gives us an assignment to see how we can write or not. Then next class he says I have good news and bad news. The bad news was we had all been screwed. Our teachers and principles did not do their jobs. The good news is that now we had Mr. Stone for a teacher and he would not advocate his responsibility like the others...."

From another student:

> "Stone was jive at the start. Talking way over our heads. So I told him in class come on man. These folks ain't getting this shit. Start at the beginning, start at first grade. Maybe I did wrong calling him out in front of everyone but he was cool. Next class he comes in with workbooks from grade school. It wasn't a class anymore but a grammar factory and we all started hammering away and helping each other."

Gabriel smiled—the writer reminded him of himself at the police academy three decades earlier. The next few entries read:

> "Prof. Stone said we must use all we learned to write this Teaching Effectiveness Evaluation Comment. No mistakes. Use the dictionary. These

will show everyone the good teacher that he is...."

"Mr. Stone always had us write about our schools and what we did there. He made me think about why things happened the way they did and the way they were supposed to happen. He made me loose sleep worrying about prepositions and past tense."

"Profesor he change my life. That is, Professor Jonathan Stone has changed my life. He has given me hope and tools I need to get thru college and be a success in life.... I love to diagram sentences! It makes you see how words all work together— nominative case and objective case, prepositions and their objects. Why did no one ever teach me this? Because of Professor Stone I am going to be a teacher and go back to teach at my school. I love Professor Jonathan Stone! ☺"

Gabriel looked up, out to the park, where more snow was again falling. Appropriately, a jazz guitar instrumental of "White Christmas" played in the background. His gaze moved to the video of the burning logs, which made him think of Dadisi's gas fireplace. Maybe this was what Dadisi had been trying to tell him. That Stone was an exceptional instructor who was dismissed not for incompetence but for some other reason, which Dadisi couldn't or wouldn't reveal. In other words someone—Betancourt perhaps—was out to get Stone for whatever reason, and they got him.

Or maybe it was just that things were different from Ga-briel's college days. He'd heard about it: lowered standards, grade inflation, feel-good education. Hardly the sort of ass-kicking instruction he had gotten from the Jesuits, et al. Apparently the rules had changed. But Stone was still playing by the old ones, and some people didn't like it.

§

Christmas morning the snowplows were out again. Gabriel restarted the fireplace video and the Christmas jazz and fetched the newspaper from the hallway. At nine his son called from D.C. Gabriel could hear his two grandkids yelping in the background. Tim told him they loved the toys he sent. Everyone was well.

"You talk to your mother?" Gabriel asked.

Tim cleared his throat. "She's here now. Visiting for the week."

"Well, give her my regards."

"You want to talk to her?"

About what? How they abandoned each other? How they broke their vows? Ground already amply covered. But his son wouldn't know about that. Janet and he managed to keep it under wraps until Tim was off to college.

"I'll give her a call later. Let me talk to the kids for a minute."

After he hung up, Gabriel stood looking out the window, coffee cup in hand. Thinking of his grandchildren—they'd both be entering first grade within a year or two—he now remembered having dreamt last night about being back in primary school. Marching single file. Having to sit quietly in a stuffy room. The smell and taste of erasers, graphite, and chalk. Maybe it was all computers now. Maybe kids didn't sit quietly or stay in line.

He sat on the sofa scanning the front page of the *St. Louis Post-Dispatch*. A story caught his eye about students fleeing St. Louis city schools, which had lost accreditation, for suburban schools. The resulting loss in revenue, said the superintendent, would cripple the struggling school district. Apparently the accreditation crisis had been going on for some time but beneath Gabriel's radar.

The article noted that Kansas City schools had also lost accreditation and the district there was selling off school buildings as students bolted to surrounding districts. Further, the State of Illinois had taken control of East St. Louis Schools, where student achievement had plummeted while the district misspent millions of dollars, legislators claimed.

His phone buzzed again—a call from the North Patrol Division. A female officer with a youthful voice, apparently low on the totem pole and forced to work Christmas morning, identified herself.

"Sorry to bother you, lieutenant, but I was told to call if anything relating to a Jonathan Stone came in."

Gabriel sat up straight. "What is it?"

"They just found his car."

"Where?'

"At the Arch."

That news brought visions of the ice-choked Mississippi to mind and a lump to his throat. Gabriel got the number of the lead detective on duty—Rebecca Sellers—and called, telling her he could be there in a half hour. He had nothing going on till later, but he tried not to think about that.

§

Gabriel waited outside his building for the valet to bring his car up from the garage. Soon his Dodge moved into the turnaround. A new kid emerged from it and held the door for him. Gabriel gave him a ten and wished him "Merry Christmas." He aimed the sedan up the boulevard and then onto the interstate toward downtown.

This was what had bothered Janet most, that they never had a "normal" family life. He often worked holidays and odd hours. Family meals were rare. When they went out, Gabriel carried his off-duty weapon. But now it was good that he could zip out on Christmas morning on a case that interested him without having to explain. Without having to deal with the guilt.

Once downtown, he drove past the Arch and down the inclined redbrick street toward the wharf. That too brought childhood memories: bricks everywhere. Redbrick tenements, schoolhouses, stores, and taverns; cobbled streets and alleys where he played; herringboned redbrick sidewalks; even his backyard: all bricks. He remembered being shocked when he first went to Chicago and saw its wood-frame homes, like a farm town.

Before he got to Wharf Street he turned into the parking garage and spied the white Mobile Crime Lab van in the far corner, which overlooked the Mississippi. As he drove nearer he saw the officers gathered round a black, five-year-old Jeep Grand Cherokee 4x4. He killed his engine, folded up his coat collar, and joined them.

The Crime Lab officer was lifting prints and Sellers, uniformed and rubber-gloved, was searching under the beige leather seats.

"What do you think, Becky?"

She turned, saw it was Gabriel, and straightened.

"Nice car. Four-wheel drive. Wish I'd had it this morning so I wouldn't have spent half an hour digging out my Escort."

"And from a professional police detective's perspective?"

She gestured toward its dashboard. "Given that the car was unlocked with keys in the ignition and no signs of forced entry, theft, or violence, I think that this parking spot is convenient to the river." She bent back to look under the front seat.

Gabriel pursed his lips and studied the Mississippi. It flowed milk chocolate here, after the muddy Missouri River joined it at the northernmost city limits. Dotted with chunks of ice, it looked like brown pudding with dirty marshmallows.

His gaze lifted to the Eads Bridge, only yards away, where a commuter train shushed into the station there. Built in 1874, the first bridge to span the river at St. Louis, it still carried motor vehicle traffic, MetroLink trains, and pedestrians, some of whom found it an apt place to bid the world adieu.

"Also convenient to the casino and the train," he said. "I don't think my man was that desperate to take the plunge."

Sellers commented without turning: "Okay. Then I can see where a bad casino-experience might lead a person to seek some fast cash by leaving the keys in the car."

"But my man wasn't a gambler."

She stood, shrugged, and tugged at the cuffs of her blue down jacket. "I see a lot of odd behavior. And this is odd. Anyway, it's not even his car, so he wouldn't directly benefit from its theft."

"It's not?" Gabriel spread his black-gloved palms. "Then what am I doing here?"

She lifted a hand. "No, it's the right car. Just not in his name. Ellen Cantrell's the owner."

"The wife."

Her eyebrows shot up. "The mayor's mouthpiece?"

Gabriel raised a finger to his lips. "Nothing official yet on this. Very hush-hush."

"Yeah, I get it."

"Let's compare any prints to those on the laptop I gave The Gecko yesterday."

"Who?"

"Never mind. You'll find them in the case file." Gabriel turned away and waved as he moved back to his sedan. "'Happy Christmas to all, and to all a good-night,'" he quoted as he retreated. But night was still a long way off.

- 7 -

From the Arch garage, Gabriel drove north on I-70 and exited at Riverview Boulevard, where the highway turned, and continued north, moving eventually onto Lewis & Clark Boulevard at the city limits. Within another ten minutes he was pulling into the plowed parking lot of the St. Louis Veterans Home.

"Merry Christmas!" This from a young woman, high school age, at the reception.

Men were already moving toward the dining room. Some ably, some with canes or walkers, some in motorized wheelchairs. Some were not much older than himself. He joined them as they cajoled the slow movers down the hallway.

Gabriel found his father sitting ramrod straight at a table by himself, coffee-skinned and bespectacled, his walker, yellow tennis balls on its feet, behind him. Despite the overheated room he wore a blue cardigan sweater over a white cotton turtleneck. Even at eighty-five, he still had the hard glint in his eye.

"Keep your knife out," he had told his son more than once. "Then no one will mess with you." It worked for him. The other vets settled in at nearby tables allowing Sergeant

Samuel Gabriel the dubious pleasure of his own company.

"Hey, Dad! Merry Christmas."

The old man lifted his chin in mute reply. Gabriel sat.

He brought his father up-to-date on Tim and his great-grandchildren as the meal was served: passable turkey and stuffing along with canned cranberry sauce, grayish green beans, and pecan pie. His father listened without comment and, when Gabriel had finished his report, changed the subject to football.

"The Rams don't look so good. They used to have some players. Marshall Faulk. Isaac Bruce. Now just ballerinas and fat boys. And they won't let them play, won't let them hit."

He had been delighted when the team moved from Los Angeles to St. Louis in 1995. He had been a Rams fan in the '50s and '60s when he spent time in California as he shuffled back and forth to Korea and Vietnam.

"You got the book I sent?"

"'NFL's Greatest Players.' You would have made a tight end, son."

"I know."

"You had the hands and the height."

"They didn't have football at Saint Louis U., remember? It was roundball that paid my way."

"Still...."

They stayed put as the others finished their dinners and moved off to the TV room and the card room. Soon Gabriel and his father were alone except for two women busing away the dishes. The old man told them to leave Gabriel's pecan pie, which he hadn't touched.

His father had not changed much with age, at least

physically. He'd put on a few pounds and lost what minimal hair he'd had. His face sagged yet remained largely unlined. Even though his legs were shot he maintained his broad chest and powerful arms, using hand weights that he kept under his bed. Even now Gabriel figured his father could still take him at arm wrestling.

"Ollie Matson."

"Huh?"

"Now there was a football player. Long before he played for the Cardinals and Rams, I saw him play at University of San Francisco when I was waiting to go to Korea. That was nineteen and fifty-one. They were undefeated but got no bowl game because Ollie was colored."

Gabriel tilted his head. "Lots of changes since then."

His father cast him a glance. "At first we had our own units. Then the Army disbanded the 24th Infantry Regiment, so we all fought and died together. Same in Vietnam."

This was one of the mental changes: Now he talked about the past and about the wars. He had refused to when Gabriel was growing up. He would be gone for months or a year at a time then show up unannounced and suddenly be part of the family again. No, not part of the family but a haunting presence in their home, moving about like a sleepwalker, as if in a trance. Quick to correct any misdeed or mistake and quick to anger, as if a caricature of a drill sergeant. Gabriel had avoided him as best he could. And always, when they saw him off at Union Station, the old man would kiss his wife and daughters goodbye then turn to his only son. "My eye is on you, boy," he'd say. Then he'd shake his hand, lift his olive-drab duffle bag to his shoulder, and step aboard the train.

"In Korea we had men, men who'd fought in World War II. In Vietnam it was different. Young fools right out of college or high school. You had to kick their butts to keep them alive."

A philosophy that Samuel Gabriel had also applied to his own son: hard love, with only the hard part apparent to a child. It had always been a shock to young Carlo when his father appeared and took charge after being feted and pampered for months by his mom, who, like most Mexican mothers, treated her son like Christ Almighty. It was why—in addition to Gabriel's skin color, which was a notch closer to his mom's light bronze than his dad's brown—that as a boy he identified more with her and clung to her.

But for all his parents' seeming differences, they displayed only affection for one another with nary a caustic word between them, at least not in front of the children. They had met at the Fairmount Park racetrack across the river from St. Louis, where her father trained horses, when Samuel Gabriel was stationed in nearby Granite City. Love at first sight that never wavered.

"You did a good job of that, Dad, with your men." And maybe even with his son.

"You have to fight the good fight to make your way. Be smart. Give it all you got. You making your way now, son? Or are they still messing with you?"

"Doing okay. Hoping to be back downtown soon."

His father snorted. "You did right. You were taking care of your people. Civilians don't understand."

"No, they don't."

"Your men are your family. You're responsible. You take

care of your people. That's why they call it service. Nothing wrong in serving. You don't forget that, Carlo."

His father, nonetheless, seemed to forget that Carlo was almost fifty-five and not fifteen.

"Yes, sir. I won't."

- 8 -

One good thing about being detached from headquarters was that he didn't have to set an alarm. No morning meeting, no bureaucratic B.S., no adult supervision. Another gray day coaxed him to sleep till nine. When he finally got to the office, Gabriel stopped by The Gecko's cubicle, where he found him navigating a laptop.

"Stone's?"

"Just got going on it. I sent you the list of officers on duty at the mayor's party. Guest list too."

Gabriel went to his office and perused the guest list on his laptop. The usual suspects: the Board of Aldermen, of course; the chief, fire chief, and acting school-board president; corporate bosses (both for-profit and nonprofit), Democratic Party bosses, the archbishop, and the Reverend Norris Pritchard, who ran a string of downtown homeless shelters; developers, bankers, news media shakers. He shrugged mentally, moved on to the duty roster for the event, and said aloud, "Aha!"

He found Bosco again at the front desk.

"Officer Boscovic!"

"Yes, sir!"

"Can you account for your whereabouts last Friday,

December 20, between the hours of eight p.m. and midnight?"

"Yes, I can, lieutenant. I was standing around bored shitless sober in the Mayfair Hotel ballroom watching the mayor and his cronies get plastered."

Gabriel lifted his laptop onto Bosco's desk. "Remember seeing this bloke?"

Bosco studied Stone's photo and nodded. "Yeah, he was there."

"Notice anything about his activities or demeanor?"

Bosco was thinking, his thick lips parted, his tongue pushing outward the side of his chiseled face. He made a great witness in court: cocksure, unshakeable, and always with telling details that others missed and lent credibility—urban warfare apparently made one particularly observant. All delivered with a Slavic accent that made him sound like a philosophy professor. Bosco raised a finger to his eye.

"He is a sly one, always seeing. Moving around the room." Now his finger described a circle. "Listening, not much talking. Always one eye on the mayor's woman."

"Mrs. Cira?"

"The other."

"You mean his press secretary, Ellen Cantrell?"

Bosco fixed Gabriel with a heavy-lidded gaze. "I mean Ellen Cantrell, the mayor's woman." He made an obscene gesture with his fist.

Gabriel blinked. "Really?"

Boscovic raised an eyebrow and tilted his head to the side as if to say, "Doubt me at your own risk."

"Interesting. Thanks."

As Gabriel walked back past The Gecko's cubicle, he

heard, "Hey, Carlo! Question...."

He stopped.

"The backgrounder you sent me said Stone was working on his dissertation."

"It's not there?"

"Is this it: 'The Masks of Mark Twain: Misidentification, Subterfuge and Disappearance as a River to Truth'?"

"Yep, whatever that means."

"Funny."

"Funny what?"

"The file hasn't been touched since September second. Doesn't seem like he was all that interested in finishing it."

§

After basketball and a steam, Gabriel left his car on the YMCA lot and walked down the alley to Olive Street. Still no sunshine. Dirty snow in the gutters. It had been a week at least and snow was still banked up in the street.

He waited for the light to change at 14th Street and sensed the warm gas wafting up from the storm sewer—unmistakably St. Louis. It smelled of the river and the limestone caves that undermined the city.

He moved on to the Central Library—a monumental white-stone building with arched entrances—and trudged up its front steps. Wasn't it just yesterday that his father showed him how to use the microfiche reader, the card catalog with its long wooden drawers, and the *Readers' Guide to Periodical Literature*? Now the dreaded nexus of research tedium was all computerized. He pulled open the heavy door and thought about all the date nights he'd spent studying with Janet. Deep history, now shunted into his personal archives.

He found Dadisi sitting at a low table in the children's library, a thick paperback opened in his lap. His two daughters turned the pages of an oversized book picturing mountain ranges, forests, and lakes. When he saw Gabriel, he closed his book and rose with effort from the child-sized chair.

"The knees. That's what goes first."

"Don't I know," said Gabriel, knocking on the wooden doorjamb as they passed into the Great Hall with its arched windows, ornate ceiling and chandeliers.

Dadisi looked up. "I love this place, man. Carnegie gave the money for it, you know. Used to have glass floors back in the stacks to let light through. My wife worked here before moving to the university library."

They stopped and Gabriel turned to him. "Can I ask a personal question?"

"Okay." Dadisi cocked his head.

"You're doing well. Why stay in East St. Louis?"

"Ah, a personal question—from a cop's point of view. Yeah, it's depressing and dangerous, but it's home. I grew up there. Those are my people. Most everyone and everything have abandoned it, but I haven't given up on it yet. I'm involved. Mayor's advisory group, board of a charter school, this and that. People are counting on me to do the right thing."

Gabriel studied him. "Me too, brother. You helped by directing me to Stone's student evaluations. Now I'm counting on you to help me some more."

"Still no sign of him?"

"We found his car at the Arch with the keys in it."

Dadisi shook his head. "I don't like that."

"Maybe it's not what it looks like. If I could get a clearer picture of his state of mind it might help me find him and put everyone's cares to rest. That's why I called."

"His state of mind? How good could it have been? He'd just been canned."

"Depends on how and why. Lots of people lose their jobs. Very few go postal or leap into the Mississippi."

Dadisi pulled out a chair at a wooden table in the bright-lit room. Gabriel sat across from him. The teacher brought his hands together at his lips as if in prayer. He stayed that way a moment, quiet, reading glasses hanging from his fingertips. Then he looked up. "Still confidential?"

"Absolutely."

"I've got a full-time gig, but it's not tenure-track. So I didn't tell you anything, okay?"

"Got it."

"I don't know all the details and some of what I know is second- or third-hand, but it's not that complicated. Stone had a junior-college transfer in his grammar class, DuWayne Hawkins. Starting forward on the basketball team, who needed to pass the course to move on to freshman comp and remain eligible. But that was somewhat in doubt. Apparently someone leaned on Betancourt to make sure Hawkins got through, and he leaned on Stone. But Stone dug in his heels."

"How do you know?"

"He came back to our office after meeting with Betancourt. I'd never seen him so angry. Seething, near tears. He said DuWayne was a second-rate player on a second-rate team and never going pro. He wasn't going to give him a second-rate education as well. He'd been passed along his whole life by people abdicating their responsibility. 'It stops here, with me,' he said. I believed him. Stone may be naïve and idealistic, but he's a man of his word. And his heart's in the right place."

"You had lunch with him last Friday?"

"Being it was his last day, I took him down the street to an Italian place."

"What was his mood?"

"Pensive, as always. Seemed like a lot stirring around inside—understandably. But if Stone was devastated by getting the sack, he didn't show it—though he never showed much. Word had gotten around that he wasn't coming back. His cover was that he was taking time off to work on his dissertation. I told him, 'You got a raw deal, man.'

"He stared at me and said: 'I'm not the victim here.'"

"Who then?" Gabriel asked.

"He meant DuWayne Hawkins."

"What happened to him?"

"You read the sports page Sunday?"

Gabriel shrugged.

"DuWayne scored thirty points Saturday night in the Quincy Holiday Tournament."

§

Outside the library, Gabriel checked his cell phone and found a text message from Detective Rebecca Sellers. As he had anticipated, the only prints found in the black Jeep— two sets, one male, one female—matched those found on

Jonathan Stone's laptop.

He dialed Laura Berkman and turned his back to the wind.

"Laura baby, where are you?"

"Board of Aldermen committee meeting," she whispered.

"Have you eaten? Meet me for late lunch?"

"Is this a date?"

"It's on me. Enter it in your diary however you want."

"Give me a half hour."

She showed up forty-five minutes later at a dark steak house a block from City Hall. Gabriel, who sat sipping red wine from a tall goblet and reading a paperback, stood as she approached. They grasped hands and brushed cheeks. Berkman sat and reached across to lift Gabriel's book from the white tablecloth.

"'*English Grammar for Idiots*'? Part of your reeducation, lieutenant?"

He motioned for her to hand it back. "Spied it on the new-books shelf at the library. Relates to my top-secret assignment."

"That's right: Literature and language, you said. Interesting reading?"

"Depends upon your mood."

"Is that supposed to be a joke, as in 'subjunctive mood'?"

"Perhaps, but it's not imperative to laugh."

She rolled her eyes. "Spare me."

A waiter came and handed her a menu. "Pricey. I am going to guess that this is more business than pleasure."

"A little of both."

"When will I ever again get a full dose of the latter?"

Gabriel reached for his wine and sniffed. "You probably

can't tell, what with the dim light and my dark complexion, that I'm blushing."

"Due to my sexual innuendo?"

"Not that but my failure to call for an encore. You see, well… I'm not good at explaining myself. Just ask my ex."

"Try, just a little. I thought our one indiscreet night was pretty hot."

"As did I."

"Yet no reprise."

He sipped more wine to buy time while he found the words. "You're a good gal, Laura, and I am one faithless cop. Again, ask my ex. Lovers I can find. Friends don't come so easy. Wouldn't want to jeopardize that with my noted fickleness and faithlessness."

She fondled her silver necklace as she considered his explanation. At last she said, "I guess that makes sense. You're probably right—woman scorned and all that. But perhaps an occasional get together between friends who know the score might be okay."

The waiter brought her a glass of wine.

"That might be more than okay," Gabriel said with a smile. He tipped his glass to hers. "Cheers."

"Maybe we should get down to business. I take it this has to do with your top-secret assignment."

"It does. This is big for me, Laura. If I can handle it right I'll be back where I belong."

"Never realized you were so ambitious."

He bit his lips, thinking.

"Not sure I am. Despite my usual line of crap, it's not about the money or the title or the perks. It's about respect. My dad was—is—all spit-and-polish, ex-military. A man I both loved and feared—and still do. He drilled it into me to be a stand-up guy. And that was my rep until that shit hit the front page. Made me look like I was some kind of depraved thug. This would be vindication for me, Laura."

"I don't see how I can help."

"I saw your name on the list of invitees to Mayor Cira's Christmas party. You go?"

"Oh, yeah. Never know what you might learn if you stay sober when others don't. Used to be more of an orderly Lebanese affair when their mob ran City Hall and doled things out under the table. Now it's a free-for all and everyone has their hand out. Hard to separate the gangsters from the politicians from the businessmen."

"I've noted some crossover myself. How well do you know Ellen Cantrell?"

"Well enough."

"Meaning?"

"Meaning she's not the warm fuzzy sort you want to snuggle with. Talk about ambitious. When she arrived on the scene fresh out of J-school she was aggressive and confident even though she didn't know a damn thing. Sometimes we covered the same stories and girl-to-girl I'd try to steer her in the right direction so she wouldn't make a complete ass of herself. Not that I ever got any thanks for it. Behind her back the newspaper people called her 'Geralda.' Didn't take her long to make anchor babe."

"Because she was a good journalist?"

"Please, we're talking television here. She looks like a leggy model."

"You're not chopped liver yourself, Laura."

"Thanks for the kosher diplomacy. I could buy the same

tits as hers but I'd still be five-foot-two."

"Rumor has it that she's been shaking those at Hizonor."

The jacketed waiter came to take their orders, and when he left, Berkman said, "That's one thing about clever people—they're never as clever as they think."

"At least not clever enough to fool you."

"I'm paid to keep my eyes open. Seems that over the past six months the mayor has been traveling a bit more and often including his press secretary in his entourage. Nothing wrong in that of course, just my observation. Maybe even justified in that he has a tough primary coming up in March against Aldermanic President Milton Jackson Holmes and any misstep could be costly. On the other hand it could be very, very bad, politically speaking, for him to be outted as a philanderer on the eve of that election."

"You pretty certain about the affair?"

She shrugged. "A powerful politician getting a little on the side? Been known to happen. God knows he tries with most anything in a skirt, yours truly included. And if you're wondering, I demurred. Bottom line, I'd be surprised if he wasn't stepping out on his wife. And Ellen Cantrell would surely top his hit list."

"Any solid evidence?"

"You mean like close-up penetration photos? Evidence in such cases a bit hard to come by, so to speak. But I keep reading the *Evening Whirl* in hopes they write something like: 'WHO is the downtown power ranger dipping his pen in city ink?'"

"Damn."

"What?"

Gabriel took a drink of wine but did not taste it. "This

complicates things."

"For you and your special assignment?"

"Maybe."

"But such things aren't an anomaly these days among politicians, CEOs, and football coaches."

"The same hormone that makes a man overly ambitious and aggressive also makes him overly horny," Gabriel added.

"Maybe. But in most cases I think the sex is a sideshow for all parties concerned. The real payback is power of one sort or another. For her, access to the mayor's inner circle, the movers, and the money. For him, the preening self-satisfaction a man takes by bedding a beautiful local celebrity. But as I have no idea what your assignment is all about, I have no way of judging if this is really a complicating factor for you."

He studied her. "Between friends and off-the-record?"

She nodded. Gabriel went on. "If I could locate a certain distraught someone who has taken a powder and return him to his wife without anything hitting the newspapers and/or the fan at a very inopportune time for the mayor's political aspirations, I would be rewarded."

"No shit? When did this happen?"

Gabriel counted on his fingers. "Five days ago."

"Well," mused Berkman, "it certainly could complicate things if the errant spouse—that is, the one who disappeared—was aware of his wife's unfaithfulness and the identity of her presumed lover. Particularly if he might file for divorce and make public certain facts that could compromise the mayor."

Gabriel smoothed a wrinkle in the white tablecloth. "Well, I guess there's one way to find out."

"How's that?"

"Ask the wife."

"Are you serious, Carlo? I thought you were bucking for promotion, not plotting early retirement."

He waved away her objection. "I've handled tougher customers than Ellen Cantrell. I might ruffle her feathers a bit but I can smooth them. Anyway, she's not my client, the mayor is."

"I'd love to be a fly on the wall when you ask her."

Gabriel laughed coldly. "Sadist."

- 9 -

After lunch Gabriel killed a few minutes at Police Headquarters catching up on City Hall scuttlebutt but learning nothing that might relate to his problem. He said his goodbyes and walked across the street to City Hall. There he passed through security, mounted the marble staircase to the second floor, and sidled through the doors of the Board of Aldermen Kennedy Hearing Room. He stood at the back. Positioned at the front on long tables were artists' renderings and a model of a proposed residential/commercial development, Stadium Towne, that would encircle the new ballpark. The mayor's pet project but not yet a done deal. It would have to get stamped by the Board of Aldermen. Meaning that public posturing and backroom dealing were about to commence and continue unabated until Election Day.

North Side aldermen, led by Milton Jackson Holmes, most likely would demand African-American investment and construction jobs at a significant level. South Side aldermen would suggest focusing on residential neighborhoods and their diminishing city services instead of dubious high-profile downtown projects designed to aggrandize the mayor and enrich his supporters. Other aldermanic fiefdoms would send up howls of protest hoping to be thrown a bone. Ultimately, once everyone got a shank to bury, things would move ahead nicely.

Ellen Cantrell, in a gray suit that did not clash with the colorful renderings, emceed the news conference, fielding questions from reporters and dishing them off when appropriate to the architects and developers. Always conscious of the TV cameras when answering, standing straight and still, she spoke in short, punchy sentences that could be easily edited into sound bites. She was a pro.

Laura Berkman sat alone in the second row perusing a press kit in her lap, looking bored, ignoring Cantrell. She always waited until the TV lights went out and the cameramen began packing up their gear before asking the serious nuts-and-bolts questions that might make someone squirm. This time they concerned financing and interest rates, languishing tax revenues, and the actual economic impact of the project—questions that Cantrell herself addressed but didn't really answer. Difficult to make projections and give hard numbers when you don't yet know who you have to pay off.

Afterward, Gabriel ambushed Cantrell in the hallway outside the conference room as the attendees exited.

"Ms. Cantrell, do you have just a minute? I have some good news and a question."

She looked over her shoulder and raised a finger toward her secretary, who melted away. Cantrell turned back. "You've located Jonathan?"

"Not yet, I'm sorry to say. But we found no foreign fingerprints inside the Jeep, just yours and your husband's. Meaning no evidence of a carjacking or such."

She blew out a breath through pursed, painted lips. "How did you get my fingerprints?"

Gabriel smiled. "Off your husband's computer."

She studied his eyes for a moment then nodded as if granting *ex post facto* permission to lift her prints. Gabriel continued:

"His prints were the only ones on the keys, nice and clear. Keys in the ignition, as if he had left the car there for you."

"For me?"

"It is your car, right? Registered in your name. Nice ride."

She shifted her weight to the other foot. "A leftover from my journalism days. You had a question for me, lieutenant?"

"Yes, I have. Please excuse me for being blunt, but there are rumors floating around City Hall that you and the mayor are romantically involved. I was wondering if you knew whether your husband was aware of those rumors."

At that moment, even though she was a white woman, she reminded him of his ex. Something about the eyes. It made him glad that he carried a Smith & Wesson on his belt and she was unarmed and not vice-versa.

"Detective…," She spat the word out like a rotten grape. "Your job is to find my husband. Not to chase malicious and unfounded rumors spread by political opponents. Stick to your job or I'll see you won't have one."

Ah, hardball. He tilted his head to the right as if in obeisance.

"I understand your anger. I'm just as sensitive as you are, Ms. Cantrell, to anyone besmirching my good name. But I'm trying to help. I thought to bring this up as a favor to you and the mayor. Malicious and unfounded rumors can be just as damaging as the truth. If someone, say, a political opponent, was shooting at my ass, I'd want to know so as to cover it.

"Secondly, if your husband had heard the rumors, no matter how untrue, it could certainly alter his mindset, perhaps dramatically—particularly coupled with losing his job. If I'm to find him I need to know all I can about what might be motivating him and his state of mind at the time of his disappearance."

She pressed the portfolio she carried to her chest. "I see what you're saying. I am worried about Jonathan. If he'd heard such rumors, he made no mention of them to me."

"To your knowledge did anything occur at the mayor's Christmas party last Friday night that might have agitated Jonathan? Maybe someone trying to get to you and the mayor through your husband."

"I don't know. I was busy. We hardly talked…" She looked down. "He's always been serious-minded, but I've never known him to be depressed or to.…" Her breath seemed to catch in her chest.

"I understand," Gabriel said. "We'll find him. He's likely just lying low and thinking things over. No one just disappears."

The usual cop crap, kin to "Help us and we'll help you" and "We're doing all we can." Phrases that make the job somewhat manageable.

§

Next morning, just like he figured, Gabriel got a call from the mayor's secretary. His phone buzzed as he stood in his robe with his coffee cup watching the sun rise over the silhouetted Arch. At times in the evening it glowed golden as the sun set behind his building. Then it looked like a great gilded handle affixed to the riverfront awaiting the hand of God to yank the city to heaven or hell.

Within the hour he was again mounting the marble staircase at City Hall. On the second floor he marched into the red-carpeted suite on the building's north side where the mayor's assistant told him to go on in, he was expected.

In the mayor's office, tall windows overlooked Market Street and the park there. A block over he could see the Soldier's Memorial with its staunch columns and beyond it another two blocks the arched entrance to the Central Library.

Angelo Cira—Mad Angelo—sat behind his desk talking on the phone, an unlit cigar seated between forefinger and middle finger of his left hand. In summertime he often wore colorful Hawaiian shirts with palm trees and such, gabardine slacks, and Italian loafers sans socks. But today it was a nice charcoal hound's-tooth suit that Gabriel envied, a French-blue dress shirt, and silk tie—navy with gray crosshatches. He was in fine form. Cira gestured with his cigar toward a chair across from him. Gabriel folded his scarf and topcoat on an adjacent chair, sat, smoothed his own tie, and pretended not to listen.

"I don't give a damn what Holmes is saying publicly. Once we've handed him his ass in the primary he'll come along ... Not to worry. I know how to take care of him ... Okay, see you then."

The mayor hung up the phone and shook his head. "Politics! People! If I could just be Dictator for a Day I'd fix everything, Carlo. Well, it might take a year or two. Just tell everyone what to do and it gets done or else. But no, everyone's got their own agenda and their own ideas. You got to wheedle and cajole the bastards to get them to lift a finger."

"I'll try not to fall into that category."

Cira laughed. "No, you're a team player, my friend. Always have been. That's why I brought you in on this."

"I appreciate it."

"I want you to push ahead as hard as you can to find this guy." Cira made a fist.

"I am."

"But just keep to the task. Don't stray."

"I understand."

"I don't want anything to hit the media at a bad time. I've got the primary in March. I need this resolved. And I need Ellen Cantrell focused on her job and not worrying about her old man."

First person singular: I, I, I. The mayor was still the same self-involved Angelo Cira he'd always known, albeit now with silver hair and mustache instead of black, tailored suit in lieu of SLPD blue.

"She doesn't seem too worried."

Cira puffed on the cold cigar and studied Gabriel with deep-set eyes. "Look, Carlo. The public's memory is about as long as my dick. By next summer they won't give a damn who you thumped or how hard. We can bring you back downtown. Put you back in place. Like old times. Maybe we can even work together again. That's what you want, isn't it?"

Gabriel sat with legs crossed, hands folded in his lap. "More than anything."

"I wanted you handling this because you know how to play ball. Find a good resolution and your ticket's punched."

The mayor's eyes moved momentarily to Gabriel's overcoat. He reached for it and stood.

"Thanks, Ange. That's good to hear."

Cira came around the desk and embraced him. He whispered in his ear. "We've always stuck together, Carlo. You're my main man."

Gabriel jogged down the broad stairs to the first floor where Preacher Cairns had cornered a young couple who had come to City Hall for their marriage license. He paused to take in the scene, which took him back to more innocent times. Then he moved outside, stood on the steps, and tightened his scarf to buffer an icy north wind blowing down the boulevard. He should have felt good about his meeting with Angelo and the sizeable carrot the mayor had dangled before him. But he didn't.

§

Back at the North Patrol Division office Gabriel found The Gecko in the kitchen coaxing the last drops out of the coffeemaker. He never quite filled out his uniform, which always hung in disarray—collar of the blousy light-blue shirt wrinkled, black nametag crooked, dark-blue tie off-center, shoes scuffed. But today it looked like he had slept in it, his eyelids red, skin oily.

"You look like hell, Gecko. You should give the little lady a rest once in a while. You'll wear it out."

The Gecko sipped from a Washington University mug. He had taken a degree at the elite local school magnum cum laude in Computer Science & Engineering. But for some reason he wanted to be a St. Louis cop instead of a Silicon Valley potentate. Go figure.

"Partying with Professor Stone—not Sarah—till four," he said, "per your instructions to bear down, lieutenant. Come. I'll show you what I found."

On the drive back to the office, Gabriel had wondered when a break might come. Stone had to be somewhere, dead or alive. Sooner or later he had to surface—figuratively or literally. The sooner the better for Gabriel's purposes. Now, maybe The Gecko had turned up something. He followed his colleague down the hallway. "Something show up on his credit cards or bank account?"

"Nothing yet."

"I'm starting to think my man's in the river. Under a log or an ice floe."

"I'm not so sure."

He sat at his desk, where Stone's laptop had been wired into his computer and oversized monitor. Gabriel pulled up a chair beside him. The computer geek began working his mouse and keyboard.

"Looks pretty innocuous, right? Emails to students, visits to online libraries, paperbacks bought at Amazon, e-books downloaded from Gutenberg. Literary subscriptions and memberships. Damn few documents. Just the abandoned dissertation and a few book reviews and articles he'd written. Which got me curious. You indicated he was conducting some educational research, something to do with the schools. His office mate Dadisi said he had become 'obsessed' with it according to your notes. But none of it was here. Which suggested it must be somewhere else."

"Brilliant, my dear Watson."

The Gecko continued typing. "So I began poring through all his web history to see the sites he'd visited. He'd cleaned it out regularly, which might have fooled most lay people. But everything you do is there somewhere on the hard drive if you know where to look. And, bingo! There it was."

Gabriel focused on the screen and frowned. "Cloud eye ex? What the hell?"

The Gecko cast him a disdainful look. "Cloud nine. An online drop-box where you can store documents and access them from any computer. He visited it only once from this laptop to set up the account. Which I have successfully hacked into. Here, lieutenant, is where Stone secreted all his research and apparently accessed from a second computer."

Gabriel read the file names aloud: "'Corruption in academia.' 'Corruption in the public schools.'... 'corruption, corruption, corruption' ... What's he up to?"

"Our man—if he's still alive—is on a mission. Some pretty enlightening reading, Carlo."

"Sounds like just the thing for the weekend—a real page-turner. Can you get me copies?"

The Gecko held up a two-inch-long leather sheath. "It's all on this flash drive, lieutenant. Good luck with it."

Gabriel took it, stood then turned back. "You said 'emails to students.' Any one such student with a lot of traffic. Female maybe."

The Gecko focused again on the monitor and began manipulating the mouse. "You have a dirty mind, lieutenant."

"I have the mind of an experienced investigator and wounded veteran in the battle of the sexes. If a guy ducks out on his wife and leaves no trail of transport, credit-card purchases, or hotel rooms, I have a hunch he's getting some home cooking."

"Let's see what we have … Most prominent email recipient is Letty NXS at gmail dot com—Leticia Tatum."

"Substance?"

"Seems mostly school bidniz as opposed to monkey bidniz. Here's an exciting one titled 'Question about the subjunctive.'"

"Sexy."

"Well, you do want to fall asleep afterward. Another asking about books she ought to be reading."

"Tone?"

"Seems friendly, lighthearted, nothing incriminating. But he is using his university email account and likely cautious if anything was going on."

"Well, the only way to learn is to ask questions. Let's email Miss Tatum."

§

The old neighborhood. "Old" in a couple senses for Gabriel. Where he grew up, within a few blocks of downtown. Comprised in large part, at least then, of antebellum flats and terraced houses dating back to the 1840s. Even up into the 1960s some still had outhouses in back by the alley and a single coldwater faucet in the kitchen sink. Now officially called the Old North St. Louis neighborhood, adjacent to the former Polish enclave centered on Cass Avenue and the old Irish neighborhood Kerry Patch, it was trying to come back, though with few signs of success. Mere blocks from the infamous Pruitt-Igoe housing project—internationally renowned for its failure and ultimately dynamited into history—the neighborhood now consisted of some rehabbed row houses, a few new townhomes, boarded and decrepit redbrick residences, abandoned storefronts, numerous vacant lots, and, of course, Crown Candy Kitchen, a St. Louis institution.

As he pulled his Dodge Charger to the curb he noticed two young black men—baggy jeans, black hoodies—on the corner eyeing him. When he stood and made a move toward them, they strode off in opposite directions. He called:

"You better run, homeslice, or I'll pat you down just for fun."

He climbed a worn limestone stoop to a rehabbed home in the middle of the block and knocked. The door opened a crack and a young black woman peered out over a chain.

"Letty? I'm Lieutenant Gabriel. I emailed you."

"Yeah?"

He showed her his badge. "I want to talk to you about someone I'm looking for."

"I don't know him."

"Who?"

"Whoever you're looking for."

"I think you do: Jonathan Stone."

She frowned. "Professor Stone? He in trouble?"

"I hope not. But maybe you can help me."

She closed the door to unchain it and stood in the jamb looking over her shoulder. Behind her a TV blared and kids squabbled. She turned back, saying:

"My sister's babysitting with school out. Pretty noisy."

"Walk down to Crown's with me where we can talk. I'll buy you a milkshake."

She looked him up and down. "Let me see that badge again."

He held his I.D. out to her once more. She looked from it to his face and back again.

"Give me a minute." She closed the door.

He stood on the herringboned brick sidewalk, his face stinging from the cold. Most of the houses on the block were gone, as if from aerial bombing. The kids, too. He and his pals were out on the streets year round. Playing football, stickball, and bottle caps, or fashioning some make-believe adventure. The girls had hopscotch, jacks, jump rope, and tag. Now there was virtually no one about. Except for the two who had scurried off as soon as he pulled up.

Five minutes passed before Letty emerged. They strolled down North 14th Street under a vague sun, she shapely in tight jeans, high-top red sneakers, and a thin black-leather jacket with sheepskin collar despite the freezing air. They passed through a rehabbed shopping district with new storefronts, benches, trees in planters, and stylish streetlamps. But most of the storefronts were empty and no shoppers were to be seen. A chill passed through Gabriel, and he turned up his collar against the north wind.

At the Crown Candy Kitchen the lunch crowd had dissipated. A North St. Louis icon that had first opened for business a hundred years earlier, it served as an anchor for the neighborhood. But Gabriel feared that wasn't nearly enough to keep it from drifting further into decay.

They sat across from each other in a booth against the wall. When the waitress came Letty ordered a chocolate banana malt with whipped cream and nuts.

"Just coffee for me,' said Gabriel.

"You sure?" said the waitress.

He laid a hand on his stomach. "Don't tempt me."

Gabriel sat looking to the tin ceiling, studying the menu on the wall behind the soda fountain, and eyeing the old jukebox nearby. "I used to come here with my wife when we were in school. Before you were born."

"You lived here?"

"On Howard. Old row house. Had to go around back and climb wooden stairs to get in. Gone now."

"I've seen pictures of the neighborhood. Looked okay then."

Gabriel saw them, too. Had lived them.

The waitress delivered Letty's malt and his coffee and then retreated.

"You fond of Professor Stone?"

"Why are you looking for him?"

"Between you and me, he hasn't been seen for a week. His wife is worried."

"So he is married." She pursed her lips around the straw and sipped at her malt. Then she lifted a bit of whipped cream from its top on her finger and licked. "He wore a wedding band, but you never know."

"But you liked him."

"I learned lots from his class. He helped me. Made me want to be a teacher. I'm going to major in English."

"What about as a woman?"

She looked down at her malt and shrugged a shoulder. "Sure. Everyone did."

"You emailed him a lot."

She looked up and leaned forward, elbows on the tabletop. "You know what it's like. Someone wants to help you, you take what you can get. Figure a way to do something. Maybe I was crushing on him, but I can get that anywhere. He knew it was there if he wanted it. But he didn't want it for whatever reason. The other—I saw he could really help me. I need to take care of me first."

"I understand."

"But he wanted something from us, too. Maybe it was for his doctorate paper—what do you call it?'

"Dissertation."

"Yeah, his dissertation. He was always asking us about our schools—our grade schools and our high schools. We were studying grammar and writing but he always made us write about that: what we did in class, what we did after school, what textbooks we had, what reading and studying we did, what sort of teachers we had. He had us write about the bad stuff, too: the fights and the troublemakers and the subs who were marking time. About the kids who came and went and you never saw again."

Gabriel ignored his coffee, focusing on Letty's malt. Its banana aroma wafted to him, taking him back to his school days and Janet.

"You said all the girls liked him. Any more than others?"

Letty smirked. "Whitney'd go up after class and shake her little titties at him. Go to his office. But he had nothing to do with her either."

"You know for sure?"

"*She* would have told everyone."

"Probably just as well then."

"If he had anything going on with anyone we would have known. You can tell. People think they can hide it but they can't."

Like Ellen Cantrell.

"Not everyone in class appreciated him as much as you did."

"Some had trouble. They couldn't get it. Or didn't want to."

"You mean like DuWayne Hawkins?"

"DuWayne Hawkins is an ass. Thought that bouncing the roundball and acting the fool was enough to get him what he wanted."

"Did he dislike Stone?"

"He didn't care one way or the other. He was dozing half the time."

Gabriel sat thinking. Sometimes his hunches bore fruit. Sometimes they didn't. This seemed like one of the latter.

Letty said, "Did I help you?"

"Yes. Helped me eliminate some possibilities."

She sipped at her malt then said: "Then can you help me?"

His eyes locked onto hers but she looked down, long eyelashes curling over her cheeks. Traffic ticket? Boyfriend in trouble?

"If I can. What's it about?"

"Find out about Alonzo."

"Who?"

"Alonzo Watkins. He was in Professor Stone's class. I saw it in the paper Saturday morning. Got himself shot over in Hyde Park."

"Killed?"

She bit her bottom lip and blinked away tears. "I don't think so. He's a nice boy. Real quiet. Paper said the mothers shot him in the back."

Gabriel walked Letty home and continued strolling on to Howard Street and the address where he grew up. Just a vacant lot now: snow-covered earth and busted bricks. He pictured his mother in the kitchen singing as she often did while going about her chores. Gabriel took in a deep breath and let it out in a cloud. Everything changes. Nothing changes.

§

Back in his office at the North Patrol Division Gabriel found a brief online *Post-Dispatch* story on the shooting incident from the previous Saturday morning—the day Stone disappeared. Alonzo Watkins, nineteen, discovered in Hyde Park after neighbors reported the sound of gunshots. Wounded once in the back. Apparent robbery— though what would a North Side college student have worth stealing? Probably a laptop. But then he had seen kids stabbed for a pair of sneakers. Watkins was taken to Barnes-Jewish Hospital, critical condition. Police were investigating.

Gabriel pulled up the department's digital case file. It revealed that Watkins had likely deboarded the #04 Natural Bridge bus at ten p.m. and was walking home on Salisbury Street. The contents of a backpack were found scattered on the sidewalk near the body: spiral notebooks, textbooks, chess pieces, and chess clock. The bullet, small caliber, had entered just left of the spine, passed below the heart— doubly lucky there—and pierced a lung. A full recovery was predicted. In a follow-up interview at the hospital the victim claimed not to have recognized any of his three assailants.

He could not or would not give a description except to say they were—surprise!—African-American males between ages fifteen and twenty-five. In other words, he was scared shitless silent. Or plotting his own justice.

Gabriel emailed what he had learned to Letty. Then he sat staring at his desktop. If Stone had read the article about Alonzo's shooting, how would it have affected him?

Gabriel's eyes fell on his library copy of *English Grammar for Idiots*, which lay on his desk. He reached for it to see what tense he was using when he asked himself the question. If he was going to find the English professor, he should start thinking like one.

- 10 -

Friday's special at the bar of the ground-floor pub in his building was fried cod. It wasn't his favorite, but he could down a few low-carb beers, chat with Alice the barmaid, and watch as the Blues skated on a TV above the back-bar mirror. He liked hockey about as much as he liked the cod, but the place had a dark, clubby atmosphere conducive to steady drinking if not clear thinking. The conversation around the bar consisted of lighthearted kvetching about the crappy hockey team, the crappy football team, the crappy weather. Standard St. Louis fare.

He finished dinner and made his way back upstairs where he found the Saint Louis U. basketball game on TV and muted the sound. It had been three decades since he'd played forward for the Billikens, and now their guards were taller than he was. He sat on the sofa with his laptop and slid in the flash drive The Gecko had given him.

In addition to the files he had downloaded from Stone's Cloud IX storage, The Gecko had copied Stone's cell-phone history from the previous four months and written an analysis: skimpy usage. Some twenty calls over the period to Ellen Cantrell's cell, half that many to Martha Walczyk at the English Department. No pattern change just prior to his disappearance. In other words, nothing interesting.

He then opened Stone's first-listed folder, "Corruption in academia." In addition to a text file, it contained three audio files. Gabriel opened the text file and read:

> This first report documents—via eyewitness intelligence—one incident of educational malpractice and corruption. Alas, it is but the tip of a dark and malevolent iceberg poised to sink American society....

Gabriel sniffed. "'Alas,'" he said aloud. And the iceberg metaphor—a bit melodramatic. He decided he needed a drink to wade through the formal verbiage and went to the kitchen for a bourbon. He settled in again and scanned the next couple pages of summary—overwritten, in his humble cop-opinion—until he came upon a sub-head:

The Instructive Case of DuWayne Hawkins

> Among the students in this correspondent's Remedial Grammar Section was one DuWayne Hawkins, a lanky youth with a wide smile that he displayed but infrequently. A recent junior-college transfer and starting forward on the basketball team, Mr. Hawkins—like the other seventeen students enrolled in the class, all of whom had gone through twelve years of "education" in St. Louis Public Schools—could not write a grammatically correct sentence except fortuitously. Issues included missing verbs ("he my teacher"), verb-noun non-agreement ("we was walking down the street"), awkward syntax,

and God-awful spelling.

But unlike most of his classmates, Mr. Hawkins showed scant interest in learning to write a simple sentence in standard English. He did little other than mock the efforts of others. When I met with him privately and questioned him on his attitude, he scorned the need to speak and write conventional English—or even to study in order to pass the course and maintain his athletic eligibility. "I'll get by," he said cryptically.

"No, you won't, not without working and learning this," I told him.

He laughed and looked down at me as if I were a poor, misguided fool—which riled me. However I soon came to learn what fueled his derisive response.

After mid-term I received an email from English Department Chair Armand Betancourt asking me to see him. When I found him in his office he asked me how DuWayne Hawkins was doing in class.

"Not well," I answered. I went on to tell Betancourt that Mr. Hawkins came to class but did little work and showed little improvement. He turned in acceptable homework assignments but didn't actively participate in group workshop-exercises. His poor performance on in-class writing assignments and quizzes led me to suspect that he harbored a grammatical Mr. Hyde who completed his homework—or had a tutor who did so.

"See that he gets through the course," said Betancourt.

"That depends on him. This isn't unscrambling

dense literary theory," I said. "It's basic grammar and writing. He has to want to learn. But he obviously doesn't."

"Then motivate him, Stone," said Betancourt. "You're the teacher. That's your job."

I thought to argue that point—that adult university students attending voluntarily, presumably in order to learn, were thus already sufficiently motivated—but understood the futility of it. "Perhaps," was all I said. But that was enough to make Betancourt grit his teeth.

"Get him through," he reiterated. "He needs a C or better. And I need Administration off my back."

That ended the conversation. I retreated to my office and transcribed it as best I could from memory. In subsequent meetings with Professor Betancourt, reported below, I carried a hidden digital audio-recorder. Thus those conversations are transcribed verbatim. Copies of those audio files can also be found in this folder. According to Missouri law, private conversations can be legally recorded with the consent of only one participant.

"You sly mother," Gabriel said aloud with a smile. He looked up to see that the Billikens had taken an early eight-point lead. He sipped his bourbon and read on:

Nonetheless, I took Professor Betancourt's admonitions to heart. For in-class exercises I paired DuWayne Hawkins with the most advanced students, hoping their enthusiasm and work ethic might infect him. It did not. I personally worked with him in class when feasible and offered to tutor him privately—an offer to which he did not respond. Once in class, when I asked him a question, he mumbled something incomprehensible.

"Mr. Hawkins," I said, "please speak up and enunciate. And try to use complete, grammatical sentences. That's what we're about here."

"How we talk."

"I know that's how you talk among your peers or at home. We all speak in dialect of one sort or another," I told the class. "But we need to know and be able to use grammatically correct English that communicates effectively with all people in the English-speaking world—which is growing globally. We're trying to expand your world and empower you."

"You making us little Honkies," said Hawkins. "So the Man keep us down."

The class laughed at that. But I found it galling.

"No, Mr. Hawkins, quite the opposite. I'm trying to liberate you. Doors are open. All you have to do is step through. But you need to check your dialect at the door. Think of it as a remnant badge of slavery—along with the attitudes that go with it, such as sullenness, sloth, and a sense of grievance. People are trying to help you, not oppress you." He glared at me and shifted uneasily in his seat. But others in the class sat up and took note, so I went on.

"My family also came to America in chains—not the literal chains your ancestors may have worn, but legal chains, as indentured servants. And I would still be a servant, doing some menial task—maybe flipping burgers—if I hadn't learned the standard language of my family's adoptive homeland.

"What I am trying to give you, all of you, is that same chance. If you can read and write well, you can begin to make something of yourself—which takes hard work."

However, my pontificating did little to change Mr. Hawkins' behavior or study habits, though most of the other students seemed to respond positively.

Then, on November 22nd, I received another email from Dr. Betancourt, again with a blank subject line and a terse message: "Pls c me." I noted that he again made no mention of the reason for the meeting, as if avoiding leaving any documentation of its substance. It was then I purchased the pocket-sized digital voice recorder.

He kept afternoon office hours, and I found him there the next day. When he saw me he said, "Close the door and have a seat." I did so. He went on: "I understand, Stone, that when queried by the Athletic Department as to DuWayne Hawkins' standing in your class you replied that he was likely to fail."

"At this point it looks like a sure thing."

"That's unacceptable. I told you to get him through."

I told Betancourt of the extraordinary efforts I took with Hawkins and how other students in the class also tried to encourage and help him but to no avail. "I did what I could. But he showed no interest at all in learning—in fact, he actively pushed back and resisted it."

Betancourt removed his reading glasses and rubbed the bridge of his nose as if to dispel a headache. "He attended class? Then he must have learned something."

"Not judging by the most recent in-class writing assignment."

"It's important that he gets a passing grade for this course."

"Important to whom? DuWayne Hawkins has been passed along his whole life. As a result he's been robbed of an education. He's been robbed of his citizenship."

"Let's not be overdramatic, Stone. Look at the big picture. Athletics, for better or worse, are an important tool for development and recruitment efforts. As academics we may not like it, but that's the way of the world these days. I tried to fight this battle before but no one's listening. I'll tell you what they told me: 'Everyone's job and well-being in the university depends on it, including yours.'"

I noted but did not comment on the implied threat. Instead I said:

"The big picture's distorted. I'm focused on DuWayne Hawkins and his future."

"DuWayne Hawkins isn't the issue here."

"I don't understand. If the student in question is not the issue, then who or what is? Our job is to educate students, students like DuWayne Hawkins. That requires standards. And integrity."

That last comment made Betancourt bristle.

"Spare me the lecture. I've given the same one myself without effect. Are you going to play ball or not, Stone?"

"Interesting metaphor in this context," I said. "The best I can do is an incomplete."

"Not good enough. He needs the credits and advancement to remain eligible. Think about it, Stone. You still have three weeks till grades are due. See that you get him up to a C."

"Are you asking me to violate departmental standards and university ethical guidelines?" I asked him.

"No," he said. "I am *telling* you to see that Hawkins achieves an acceptable level of performance to merit a C grade. I'm under enough pressure. Don't make it worse."

Eyes glued to the computer screen, Gabriel reached again for his bourbon. Stone would make a good witness—if there was a crime.

I had one last private conversation with Betancourt on the morning of my final day in the English Department. I found him in his office, strode in, and closed the door behind me.

"Open the door, please," he said.

"This is a personnel discussion. Confidential matters, not public discourse."

"What's it about?"

"First and foremost DuWayne Hawkins. You changed his grade."

"What knowledge would you have of that?"

"You know damn well I have none. After I submitted my grades, I was locked out of the system."

"Standard security for former employees."

"Speaking of which, you weren't even man enough to tell me face-to-face I was being fired."

"Call it what you will, Stone."

"I call it cowardly. You expect me to find another job in three weeks?"

"You knew the stakes. We need team players here."

"We need educators committed to their profession, not the politics of personal advancement."

Betancourt fumed. I had learned he was vying to become dean of Arts and Sciences.

"Your arrogance and insubordination annoy me, Stone. You have all the moral superiority and answers, including how best to educate black students without knowing the first thing about it."

"I don't see what race has to do with it. Are you saying black students learn differently or need lower standards? I find that view racist."

"Get out." Betancourt reached for the phone. "I'll call security if I must."

"Call your mother if you want, you little prick. And besides, fuck you."

I left. I wasn't proud of those last comments—my wild Irish roots showing. But I had been under some stress personally as well as professionally and at that point figured I had nothing to lose.

§

His buzzing cell phone pulled Gabriel from his laptop. The caller ID read: GECKO HOME. He answered and heard:

"Some shoddy police work to report, Lieutenant Gabriel. A 911 call Saturday night that didn't get properly logged. Came in at 9:28 p.m. Cell call of a jumper off Eads Bridge."

"Confirmed?"

"No confirming call and no answer on the callback. On the audio file the caller sounds like a black female, young. By the time a unit showed up, the caller had left—if she was ever there in the first place. The river had chunks of ice floating in it. Patrolmen figured maybe the caller thought she saw someone in the river. Or more likely it was a prank call. And no one at MoDOT was monitoring the bridge cameras that time of night. Not much to be done at that point. If there was a jumper and the fall didn't get him, the freezing river would."

Gabriel thanked him and hung up. He felt sick to his stomach. Stone seemed like a decent guy. He deserved better. Much better.

- | | -

Saturday morning Gabriel woke in a funk. He'd drunk too much and hadn't slept well. The Stone case was getting to him.

Most of his career he had dealt with serial criminals and screw-ups, people who had chosen a degenerate way of life for whatever reasons. Generally the two things those career criminals held in common were substance abuse and ignorance—at least the ones who got caught. Some saw the light in prison and managed to straighten their lives out, and some were just irredeemably fucked up. Some ultimately got killed in jail or on the streets.

But coping with Stone—a bright guy who, again for whatever reasons, hadn't been as successful as he likely should have been and who had been wrestling with frustrating and humiliating issues both at home and at work that led to his apparent suicide—was dispiriting.

Further, Gabriel had to contend with City Hall ball-busters—people who held his future in their hands, and squeezed. Then there were the institutional failures: a dedicated teacher fired for adhering to standards, black kids not being properly educated.

He knew things were difficult in the schools. For years

he'd dealt with juveniles who got in trouble. If they could read and write then, as Stone argued, there was hope for them. If not, they were lost. And each year more and more hit the streets—dropouts with scant skills and dim prospects, many who turned to crime and drugs.

But raising them right and teaching them was not a cop's job. Over the years he had gone to the schools to lecture about the dangers of gang involvement and the importance of law and order to the community; he'd worked with juvenile officers when there was an issue and then, when kids messed up, he'd run them down and kick their ass in hopes of staving off more serious crimes. He sensed that Stone had felt a similar calling—to kick butt so they could write a decent sentence.

Gabriel's mood could hardly be worse.

He telephoned the North Patrol Division and rechecked regional reports: No one had been pulled from the Mississippi. It had been a week since the call about the jumper. The body—if there was one—most likely was snagged on a bank in South St. Louis or cruising past Natchez, Mississippi. That thought did nothing for his mood either.

He considered calling Ellen Cantrell with the news about the Eads Bridge jumper, but that idea made his stomach churn. It was a part of the job he always hated. Bringing people bad news about a family member and having to deal with their grief, if but momentarily, disturbed him more than it should have. It wasn't that he was a bleeding heart. He had no problem arresting, subduing, or even shooting some asshole. But seeing innocent people hurt was something else.

Gabriel finally decided that there was no point in

upsetting Ellen Cantrell on the basis of an unsubstantiated report that the attending officers found dubious, even if he himself didn't.

He thought about driving downtown to the Y for basketball—there were usually some better players on Saturday mornings. But what he really needed was some fresh air.

He donned pressed blue jeans, clipped his Smith & Wesson to his belt, and pulled on galoshes, overcoat, and stocking cap. Though he was no longer required to carry a pistol when off duty, he felt light without it. Even at the Y he had it in the gym bag that he carried to the basketball court, not trusting to leave it in a locker.

Gabriel took the elevator down and crossed the boulevard to Forest Park, where the six-mile-long bike path encircling it had been plowed. He strolled through Kennedy Forest to the art museum.

Its north façade overlooked Art Hill, where hundreds of kids and adults rode sleds, toboggans, plastic discs, and flattened cardboard boxes down the long, snow-packed slope to the frozen Grand Basin, cordoned by hay bales. A chaotic scene, with those climbing up the hill dodging those hurtling down. Two large, smoky bonfires burned atop the hill, where children and adults alike gathered to warm their hands before careening back down the hill again.

He recalled speeding down the hill with his son and then, earlier, when he was a boy, on his Champion sled, sitting between the legs of his father, who seemed to enjoy it as much as he did. His mother, who had grown up in sultry Jalisco, remained by the bonfire, encased in coat, scarf, mittens, and wool cap. Now he heard Spanish, English, black dialect, and—coming from an Indian family—what he took to be Hindi, as well as other tongues. Some Muslim parents, judging by the hijabs the women wore, speaking—what? Arabic? Farsi? Urdu? A different, more cosmopolitan city from some fifty years earlier when he started school at Most Holy Trinity. Then most everyone spoke English.

At first it was nuns for him. Brothers later in high school. Jesuits running Saint Louis University. All were exacting, on task. As Stone had told Dadisi, writing a grammatically correct sentence was something most kids back then accomplished in the first grade. How could someone go through twelve years of school and not be able to do it by graduation? No discussion then of race or special treatment for Gabriel and other black kids, albeit he was a racial mixture in a racially mixed school. Everyone was held to the same standards in the classroom and out. Kids who needed extra help got it, black, white, or Hispanic, though the last were rare then. Race came up at times, usually when angers flared between boys competing on the playground. But any racial pejorative that landed on a teacher's ears was quickly corrected and punished. On the streets, the kids applied their own brand of correction.

Enough reminiscing. And enough of the cold. He turned to head back home to read Stone's entries. But the thought of it all weighed on him. Not only because of what he was sure would be lugubrious subject matter, but also because he didn't relish passing his day communicating with the dead. Nonetheless, until he heard otherwise, Stone was still missing and his job was to find him, dead or alive.

§

Gabriel sat at his dining table with his laptop and a cup of coffee, looked out to the snowy park one last time, and opened the file titled "Corruption in the public schools." It began with a quote from Mark Twain: "Every time you stop a school, you will have to build a jail."

Culling information from numerous sources, Stone painted a grim picture of St. Louis schools—not that they were that exceptional. Kansas City's and East St. Louis's were even worse, he contended.

The failing schools were depressing already low property values and contributing to neighborhood disintegration and crime. Both St. Louis and Kansas City Schools had recently lost accreditation. Students were fleeing en masse to other districts, charter schools, and private schools.

In St. Louis they were escaping a school system where children quickly fell below reading and math standards. Recent graduates, presumably Stone's grammar students, recalled frequent fights, low attendance, and low standards. Half the students would never graduate.

Many feared gang activity in and around the schools. Other reasons for dropping out included pregnancy, apathetic parents, incarceration, disciplinary problems, and repeated academic failures. In St. Louis alone, hundreds dropped out each year, swelling the number of at-risk youths on the streets. Nationally, seventy percent of state-prison inmates were dropouts, wrote Stone.

Gabriel skimmed the lengthy document—it ran some twenty thousand words including copious endnotes—and focused on its conclusion.

The learning crisis in American inner-city public schools (though it exists in varying degrees in poor rural and suburban districts as well) amounts to widespread educational malpractice. Over the past forty years academic achievement has plummeted while education expenditures per student have doubled....

Gabriel turned off his computer. His gaze lifted to the park outside. In his mind he saw the kids sledding on Art Hill. If Stone was right, an educational crisis festered without concerted action to alleviate it. Which made Gabriel's job tougher. More and more discouraged and vulnerable teens on the street, more anger, resentment, gang activity, and mayhem.

But right or wrong, Stone's well-meaning idealism and pontificating didn't get him far. Just a pink slip and a plunge.

- 12 -

Monday morning Gabriel was at his desk at the North Patrol Division when he got a call from downtown. A Mississippi towboat crew had discovered a body wedged against a barge in South St. Louis. The corpse, white male, had already been transported to the city morgue. He sipped his coffee, feeling it eat at his stomach.

Gabriel drove downtown, parked his car on the street across from Police Headquarters and walked down the block in chill morning air. Now called the Office of the Medical Examiner, the city morgue, a squat, two-story building of white stone, sat behind City Hall on Clark Street, two doors down from headquarters.

He detested dead bodies, detested going there. The last time was the warm October evening when he walked the half block from his office to see his detective, Baker, who had been shot and had left behind a wife and three young children. Light brown like Gabriel, Baker looked alive as he lay naked on the gurney. But when Gabriel impulsively grasped his hand, its chill carried through him and down his spine like iced electricity. Afterward, he walked back to headquarters where the suspect was under arrest and 'rang up long distance.' Wrong number—which landed him in the North Patrol Division.

Now once again inside the building, Gabriel was greeted by an autopsy tech, a young woman named Kolb. She took him into the cooler in the southwest corner of the first floor, where dozens of white-sheeted bodies lay on gurneys—manila toe tags for most, red tags for homicide victims. The atmosphere didn't exactly smell bad. But there was something in the air that suggested death.

"Your guy's in the freezer. Wait here a minute and I'll get him," Kolb said.

He waited. Light came from outside through glass-block windows and from fluorescent lights on the ceiling. In the right corner was a body scale where gurneys could be wheeled. Behind him a curtained area, on the other side of which was a window where people came to view and identify the dead. The air felt a few degrees warmer than outside.

He moved toward the gurney that Kolb rolled from the freezer. Under the sheet was the outline of a body. She pulled the sheet back to reveal a black body bag.

"I did the blood blotter for DNA before we put him on ice," she said.

"That may not be necessary. I think I can I.D. him."

"You think so?" she said, zipping open the black bag.

Gabriel winced. "What the hell happened to his face?"

She shrugged. "Likely got chewed by a tug prop. The river's treacherous: snags, eddies, undertows. Not uncommon for a swimmer, dead or alive, to get sucked under a barge."

"Blond?"

"More or less."

"Fingerprints?"

"Dubious. Looks like something's been chewing on them as well or that he was trying to grab onto something. You might get partials."

"Right. Carry on."

Gabriel turned and moved back outside.

He walked across Clark Street and entered City Hall. Upstairs at Ellen Cantrell's offices her secretary told him she was out. He glanced up at the portrait of Angelo Cira on the wall and took a breath. He had wanted to get this part over with.

"Where can she reach you?"

Gabriel frowned. "I'd like to see her in person. This would only take a few minutes."

The man made a note. "I'll see what I can do and call you."

Gabriel walked over to Locust Street and the YMCA, where he picked up a game with downtown workers and junior execs. It felt good to jog up and down the court even though the other players were weak. He let them do the shooting just to keep it competitive. Usually this was the best therapy, physically and emotionally. But today it was hard keeping his head in the game. The image of the mangled corpse in the morgue kept slipping back into consciousness.

He was getting a massage when his phone buzzed. The masseur handed it to him. Ellen Cantrell, he was told by her secretary, could see him in fifteen minutes but just for a brief meeting. If he couldn't make it then he'd have to wait till tomorrow.

He hung up feeling sorry for Jonathan Stone, dead or alive. His wife was a real ball-buster.

§

That thought resurfaced as he sat outside her office, where he had now been waiting for twenty minutes after throwing on his clothes and dashing over like a mad man. Throughout his years of dealing with people in positions of higher authority, that sort of thing happened not infrequently: hurry-up-and-wait, cancelled appointments, general rudeness. He suspected they did it in part out of genuine indifference to the desires of underlings but also as a way of flexing their bureaucratic muscles. It made them feel good to screw with you, to remind you of their status and your place. He'd probably done it himself when he'd had some clout. If he got some of that clout back, he'd think twice before using it like this again. Just petty bullshit.

Finally the secretary told him to go in.

Overcoat over his arm, he closed the door behind him and marched toward her desk stone-faced. Alerted by his serious demeanor she stood reflexively.

"You've found Jonathan!"

She looked haggard, as if she'd had a hard weekend or was under a lot of stress. Understandable given the fact that her husband had not been heard from for ten days.

"I hope not, Ms. Cantrell."

She brought her hand to her mouth and sat. Gabriel perched on the armchair across from her.

"Two developments over the weekend: First, we learned that the night of your husband's disappearance, that Saturday, there had been a 911 entry that was misfiled. A cell call from Wharf Street of a jumper off Eads Bridge…"

That hit home: a tightening of the eyes and a gaze inside.

"…But it seemed the call may have been a prank or a mistake. There were no witnesses present when our unit arrived and no confirming reports. Which is why I didn't bother mentioning it to you earlier."

She sat staring at her desktop.

"Then just this morning I learned that a body was pulled from the river near Gasconade Street yesterday."

She brought her hand up to cover her eyes.

"A fair-haired white male, but difficult for me to identify just now as the body suffered some damage. Perhaps you could still identify him or determine that it's someone else. But we'd probably want to run a DNA match nonetheless."

Hand still over her eyes she asked: "What kind of damage?"

Gabriel swallowed. A question he had hoped she wouldn't ask.

"From a boat propeller apparently. I'm afraid the face is gone as well as fingerprints. Other cuts too."

He heard her gasp. After a moment she said, "Do I have to see that?"

"No, we can just run the DNA check. We'll put a rush on it so we're not in limbo. But we'd need to get a sample from your home—a strand of hair, fingernail clipping or whatever."

"Do what you need to do," she said without looking up. "My secretary has a key."

Gabriel rose. Not only did he dislike this part of the job, he was lousy at it. She might be a bitch and morally culpable in her husband's death, but he still wanted to put a fatherly arm around her. He didn't know what to do or say.

"Sorry to come to you with this. Let's pray it's not him."

When she did not respond he turned and walked from the room.

Gabriel made arrangements with her secretary and the Mobile Crime Lab to get a DNA sample from the couple's apartment. Then he checked his cell phone, which he had felt vibrating in his pocket while talking with Ellen Cantrell. A text message from The Gecko: "I need to see you in person."

The Gecko was a digital guy, into emails, cell calls, et cetera. Curious, the face-to-face request.

- 13 -

Back at the North Patrol Division he found The Gecko at work in his cubicle, with Stone's laptop hooked up to other computer equipment on his desk. Gabriel lowered himself into a chair and said, "What's so important, my friend, that I have to come in and look at your ugly face."

The Gecko continued staring at the large monitor in front of him. "I got curious, lieutenant. I had a feeling that this Stone character was screwing with me—or with someone. Or maybe just showing off. He was smart enough to hide the cloud account in a way that non-geeks would never find it. But there was still a clear trail to it that wasn't that hard for me to follow—a trail that he could have covered better if he knew what I think he knows and if he knew people might be looking for him. Or maybe he was just amusing himself. Or maybe he was leading me by the nose—away from something he *really* didn't want me or anybody to find. Which pissed me off."

"Go on."

"So I spent the weekend digging back into his files. And, lo and behold, I came upon this, buried in the Cloud IX account: coded info referring to a file called 'The Eddy.' Took me a while to understand what he meant, but I finally figured it out: Like an undertow in the river, the thing around which everything else is turning and getting sucked in. In other words, another cloud account with pivotal information but at another provider. It took me awhile to crack the code, but I finally did and traced his trail to the second cloud."

Gabriel let out a breath. "Not sure it makes much difference now, Geck. Looks like he may be the swimmer at the morgue."

The Gecko turned to him, eyes searching Gabriel's face. "Then, Carlo, it could make all the difference in the world."

"What you mean?"

The Gecko stood, looked over the top of his cubicle walls to see if anyone was in earshot, and bent toward Gabriel. He whispered, "Maybe he knew too much."

Gabriel laughed and slapped The Gecko's biceps with the back of his hand. "You're watching too many old movies, my man. I got this baby wrapped up. I'm on way back downtown."

The Gecko gave him a curious look. "All right, Mr. Ace Detective. You'll understand it when you read it. And for the official record, I did not read it. I have no idea what's in it."

Gabriel took the flash drive offered him and stood. "I'll go look at it."

The Gecko grabbed his arm. "Maybe better to study it at home, lieutenant. And just leave it on the flash drive. Don't save it to your hard drive."

"Do tell me why not."

"For your own good."

Gabriel smiled. The Gecko wrote a phone number on

a notepad resting on his desktop, tore off the sheet, and handed it to Gabriel.

"What's this?"

"A safe cell-phone number," he whispered. "And don't use yours if you need to talk to me about this. Go to a public phone or something."

Again Gabriel laughed. "What's with all the cloak-and-dagger, Gecko? If you're afraid, call 911."

§

It was seven o'clock by the time Gabriel got home that evening thanks to a case he got called in on because of his homicide chops. Leslie Hardaway, a seventeen-year-old honor student at the college-prep magnet school, had been found strangled when her mother got home from work. A lovely girl, he saw when he went to the Penrose Street crime scene, who reminded him of his wife at that age.

A jealous ex-boyfriend, nineteen, a dropout, finally copped to it after Gabriel kept hammering at him—figuratively. "She was the only beautiful thing I ever had," he said.

Of course the confession did little to console the girl's mother. A fucking waste all around—two lives at least. And who knows what Leslie might have done with hers....

He got a light beer from the fridge and called downstairs to the Town Hall Tavern to find out what the special was: meatloaf. They'd send a tray up. "Hold the mashed."

Gabriel sat at the table in the dining alcove and turned on his laptop. He inserted the new flash drive The Gecko had given him and saw a list of alphanumeric files and, last, a file titled, "The Eddy." He opened it and read.

The Eddy

I have no one to talk to, no one in whom I might confide all the sordid details, so I talk to myself here. Maybe I'll write a novel about it someday. It has all the dramatic elements: love, betrayal, mystery, and, perhaps, vengeance. But I can't think of her without making myself sick. I see her as I'm taking her from behind. And there, faint in the glow of moonlight coming through our bedroom window, I spy a fine line, the merest scratch, running across her buttock. And a second. Fingernail marks.

Epiphany came a bit early this Christmas season. Cognitive dissonance earlier in play, with my subconscious covering all the evidence so my conscious mind didn't have to face a painful truth. Late nights, the sudden trips out of town. The attitude, the coolness in bed, the sniping—all new. Nagging me about my dissertation, my job, my perceived lack of ambition.

I took my marriage vows seriously, made before God and man at St. Francis Xavier. Just as I took my professional duty seriously—which also cost me. Now I wonder what my civic duty is and if I have the balls to send her and Angelo Cira to prison—and whether duty trumps the loyalty a man should have toward his wife. And whether I can pull it off. And if those who play hardball downtown could stop me …

The doorbell rang and Gabriel rose from the table. Alice stood in the carpeted hall with a tray holding silverware and two dishes covered by metal lids.

"Bachelor-cop special," she announced.

He had her set it on the dining room table, signed the tab, and handed her a five. "Thanks, babe. What time the Billikens on?"

"Starts in a half hour."

"I may be down later."

He sat before his dinner tray, sliding his laptop off to the side. He read while eating.

Which is why I took care to put all this in cloud storage, where it would not be found. Including this confessional Eddy file, which is largely irrelevant anyway. I've made my confession.

I am not proud of spying on Ellen. Putting a tracking device in her car. Installing a keystroke monitor on her laptop and surveillance software on her cell phone. I did it in a fit of rage and sorrow. I went looking solely for confirmation of her infidelity, not expecting to find incriminating emails and leads concerning kickbacks and money laundering. But I felt so vengeful—which caused me to dig further. Put horns on a man's head and you put murder in his heart, it's said. Funny how killing her seems less objectionable morally than divorcing her (my formerly dormant Catholicism rising)—and more gratifying.

Gabriel scanned the page, scrolled down a few more, and

saw the narrative continuing chronologically. Their college days together. Her first TV appearance on the Mizzou station in Columbia. Graduation. Her getting the TV job in St. Louis. The Eddy ran some two hundred pages.

Gabriel went back to the list of files. He opened the first, titled "0001 – Ghosts." Like Stone's document on "Corruption in the public schools," this too began with an epigraph from Mark Twain: "The government of my country snubs honest simplicity, but fondles artistic villainy."

He read on:

At least five "ghosts" work in the offices of elected St. Louis City Treasurer Maurice Townsend, who has held the post for some 30 years. That is, employees who appear on the payroll but never appear in the treasurer's office. They include Theresa Cira Genovese, sister of Mayor Angelo Cira. The combined annual salaries of these ghosts total nearly $500,000. For three years Genovese's salary—$137,000 annually— came from funds earmarked for the Inspire Charter Schools, which are slated to close at the end of the school year due to financial difficulties....

Union organizer Thomas Welch has "worked" for the treasurer for more than 20 years, heading an "external mobile squad" charged with overseeing parking-meter operations. Welch, however, maintains his primary residence in Boca Raton, Florida, where there are no City of St. Louis parking meters. Another ghost worker, Democratic Party operative Joseph Saleem, purportedly runs the Treasurer's Office information-technology security unit, despite having no training in the field and remaining unknown to workers in the office. IT security remains lax, as I have documented here via departmental personnel files of the ghost workers, 0001.1 through 0001.5...

Gabriel found those files and peeked in: as advertised, with names, addresses, Social Security numbers, and salaries. Yet nothing too surprising. Political spoils in St. Louis? Featherbedding? Shocking!

He moved on to file "0002 – Laundry."

This and associated files document an ongoing money-laundering scheme that has worked to illegally finance local and state political campaigns. Among those implicated are former Missouri Governor Alfred "Skip" Woolrich, St. Louis Mayor Angelo Cira, Central Insurance CEO Thomas Pelletier, and Katherine Hinds, managing partner of the law firm Katz Mellon Shenk, where Cira, a former cop, practiced law after his stint as prosecutor and prior to his election as mayor.

One example of the scheme, Gabriel read, involved payments from Central Insurance Company, the insurance carrier for numerous city operations, to Katz Mellon Shenk for non-existent legal services. The law firm would then funnel the money into party campaign-coffers. This simple reimbursement ploy was repeated time and again, with money coming from various businesses seeking city and state contracts paid to various law firms.

In other words, business as usual. Though the details were

interesting. Something that the FBI might find thought-provoking. He moved on to file 0003, titled "Undertow."

> St. Louis Chief of Police Arthur Donnewald has participated in an ongoing scheme with Mound City Towing, which owns a monopoly on towing and impounding vehicles for the St. Louis Metropolitan Police Department, by which he has profited hundreds of thousands of dollars over seven years.
>
> The company falsified titles, which enabled it to sell impounded cars at inflated prices. From its sales revenue it kicked back thousands to Donnewald monthly. Further, it sold impounded vehicles to Donnewald family members at prices far below market value....

Some of this was not news to Gabriel. The previous year Donnewald's nephew had been arrested after leaving the scene of an accident when drunk. The car he had been driving, news media reported, had been purchased by his father—Donnewald's brother-in-law—from Mound City for half its street value. The police chief denied any knowledge, and the incident soon moved off the front page. But the kickback scheme, if true, was something that could bring the chief down.

The last set of files, "0004 – Play Ball," told Gabriel something of even greater interest—and of greater potential political damage.

> The developer of the $850 million Stadium Towne project adjacent to the new baseball park has made

payments in excess of $1 million to St. Louis Mayor Angelo Cira through Cayman Island bank accounts. Below you will find written and audio confirmation culled from emails, phone calls, and live conversations with Cira's press secretary Ellen Cantrell, who also stands to profit from the scheme. For over a year, she has maintained a secret bank account, previously unknown to her husband, which holds a balance, as of December 7, of $457 but has seen a flow-through of more than $800,000 in the past six months. If re-elected this spring and able to see Stadium Towne become a reality in his next term, Cira hopes to earn some $10 million in kickbacks from the project, it has been rumored, though that is unconfirmed at this point.

"Holy mother!" Gabriel leaned back and let out a long breath. His half-eaten meatloaf had grown cold. He went to the kitchen for a bourbon muttering, "Fucking Gecko."

Gabriel stood at the windows and gazed out over the park. The moon hung nearly full, laying long shadows from the naked trees across the white snow below. On the east side of the park Ellen Cantrell, newly widowed, likely slept. Miles beyond he spied the spotlighted Gateway Arch looming over the Mississippi River, from which a mutilated Jonathan Stone had recently been taken.

Had Stone's scraped fingers and chopped face come by a chance encounter with a river tug after his apparent—and possibly instantly regretted—suicide plunge? Or was there a more sinister explanation? Whichever, Gabriel wanted no part of it. All he wanted was his old job back. That and, more immediately, a decent night's sleep. Now both seemed in doubt.

- 14 -

Such an odd dream. Saint Francis Xavier College Church on the Saint Louis University campus, where Jonathan Stone and Ellen Cantrell were married—and where Carlo Gabriel had married Janet Crayton thirty years past. But in it Gabriel was not the groom but the priest, attempting to perform a wedding ceremony for a cadaverous couple reminiscent of Mexican sugar-art skeletons, though executing the task ineptly. He mumbled a few words of Latin, saw it wasn't working, and began to sing, "Take Me Out to the Ball Game." That seemed to satisfy everyone as the wedding guests began singing along and swaying to the music.

Funny. But he wasn't laughing.

As he was making coffee something else from the dream surfaced: Out the corner of his eye as he stood facing the grisly bride and groom he saw a blond man—Stone?—slip into one of the confessionals that lined the north wall of the sanctuary. That somehow adhered to something he had read the night before.

Gabriel went to his computer and reopened "The Eddy." He found the phrase "my dormant Catholicism rising" and then what had connected subconsciously for him: Stone referring to the "confessional" Eddy file, "which is largely irrelevant anyway. I've made my confession."

He called The Gecko.

"You in the office?"

"Of course. It's ten o'clock. Where are you? Starting New Year's Eve early?"

"No, overslept. But I need you to check something on Stone's computer. Any emails to or from 'Arch StL dot org'?"

"Why would he be writing to the Arch?"

"Not the fricking Gateway Arch, my benighted Hebrew friend, but the St. Louis Archdiocese. Or anything to or from a priest. May I suggest the word 'Father' as a possible search object? Call me back."

By the time he was finishing his first cup of coffee his phone buzzed. The Gecko had found something.

"You've already forwarded them to me? Good."

In his inbox were emails between Stone and a Father Michael Mohan at Saint Louis University. Gabriel wrote Mohan a brief note, saying he'd like to talk concerning the disappearance of Jonathan Stone.

Within minutes his phone was buzzing again.

"This is Father Mohan. What's this about Jonathan Stone?"

"His wife's concerned. She hasn't seen him in over a week. I was wondering if I could meet with you and chat for a few moments."

After a pause came the response: "I guess so. But I really have nothing to tell you."

Though something in the priest's voice made Gabriel doubt that.

§

He motored down Forest Park Parkway. Another frigid day. Still snow on the ground. Recent winters had been mild. This season was just ten days old and he was freezing his ass off.

Gabriel parked at a meter on Lindell Boulevard near Saint Francis Xavier and crossed the street to Jesuit Hall. At the reception desk in the lobby a gray-haired man telephoned Father Mohan's room and told him Carlo Gabriel awaited him.

"He said he'd be right down."

On the wall behind Gabriel hung a framed photo of Pope Francis. To the right of that a larger-than-life oil portrait of St. Ignatius Loyola by a 17th century Flemish painter, apparently brought to St. Louis from Belgium by Father DeSmet in the 1830s. Ancient history by Missouri standards.

His gaze was drawn outside by a bus pulling to the curb. A thin old black woman got off, bent into the wind, and scooted away.

"Lieutenant Gabriel."

Gabriel turned.

"I'm Father Mohan." Fortyish, muscular, sandy-haired, he wore gray sweats. His face—freckled, with a broad nose and fine lines at the eyes—remained rigid as they shook hands.

"Carlo Gabriel. Where can we talk?" Mohan motioned with his head toward leather wingchairs in an adjacent marble-floored lounge adorned with artificial potted plants. As they sat, Gabriel began: "We noted that you and

Jonathan Stone exchanged a number of emails, the last on Saturday the twenty-first, the day he disappeared, arranging a meeting." When the priest made no response, Gabriel went on: "Did you meet?"

Mohan nodded.

"Can you tell me what you talked about?"

"No."

"Why not?"

"Jonathan wanted me to hear his confession."

"Can you tell me anything he might have said outside the confessional? What about his state of mind?"

He shook his head. "Sorry."

"His emails indicate you had previous meetings. Anything you can say about those?"

"I'm afraid I can't help you."

The priest sat stiff.

"I sense that you can help me, Father, but choose not to. Why is that?"

"Frankly, I don't trust you, lieutenant."

Gabriel nodded. "Fair enough. I think I know why, and you are right to be cautious. Let me lay my cards on the table—full disclosure—and maybe we can build some trust."

"You are welcome to try."

"I fear Jonathan Stone may be dead. Some hours after meeting with you on the twenty-first he parked his SUV in the garage at the Arch and left the keys in the ignition. A half hour later 911 got a call of someone jumping into the Mississippi from Eads Bridge. This past Sunday a mutilated body—prop damage, apparently—was pulled from the river in South St. Louis. We're awaiting DNA results."

The priest tightened his grip on the arms of his chair. Gabriel continued:

"We also found Stone's computer files—the ones he perhaps meant us to find *and* the ones he didn't."

Mohan now leaned forward, elbows resting on his knees. "Are you Catholic, lieutenant?"

"Lapsed."

"Then you know I can't say anything about what he may have told me in the confessional. But I can tell you one thing: Jonathan Stone did not kill himself."

"He'd lost everything he had. Yet he didn't seem depressed when you last met?"

"Yes, he was certainly melancholy. But he would not commit a mortal sin."

"You sure?"

"Dead certain. Besides, he had not lost everything. If anything, his suffering had enlightened and ennobled him, as it tends to do. If he died at someone's hand, it was not his own."

"You know the powder keg he was sitting on?"

No comment.

"I am going to assume you do: that Stone had stumbled upon some highly sensitive information."

"Which is apparently your primary concern."

Gabriel felt himself flush. "Look, Father. I'm just a cop trying to do my job."

"What is your job, Mr. Gabriel? Whom do you serve? The people? Your bosses? God? Yourself? You see why I can't trust you? Not until I know the answer to that question."

It was a question for which he had no ready answer.

When he got up to go the Jesuit did not rise. By way

of parting the priest said, "I'd love to hear your confession sometime, lieutenant."

Gabriel stopped and looked at him then turned away without speaking.

§

As usual, Alice was behind the bar in the pub at Gabriel's apartment building. The place was packed for New Year's Eve. Frank Sinatra crooned about strangers exchanging glances before hooking up and falling in love as Gabriel leaned on the bar with his hand around a highball. Behind him two couples danced in front of the jukebox.

"Hello, stranger. Happy new year."

He turned toward the voice to find Laura Berkman in a black beret and overcoat.

"Same to you."

They touched cheeks, and he helped her with her coat. She wore a black cocktail dress and high heels.

"Basic black looks good on you. Out styling?"

"Trying to blend into the zeitgeist while making the rounds. My fourth and final party."

"Such as it is. What to drink?"

He gestured toward Alice, who brought her a brandy. Gabriel and Berkman touched glasses and drank. As he set his drink down, he felt her eyes on him.

"In your email yesterday, Carlo, you seemed a bit more ebullient than I'm reading right now."

"I've been somewhat dis-embullied over the past twenty-four hours."

"Your City Hall case?"

He took another sip of his bourbon and soda. "What else?"

"What did you step in this time?"

"Thought I had everything wrapped up. But issues have arisen."

"What sort of issues?"

"All sorts. Political, of course. Moral, spiritual, legal, grammatical. You name an issue, I'm dealing with it."

"Let's start with the political. That's what I'm best at."

Behind him, more people started dancing as Earth, Wind and Fire sang "September."

"How clean, in your estimation, is Angelo Cira?"

On the TV above the bar the New Year's countdown had begun. Berkman shrugged. "Crooked as hell, but at least he's upfront about it. Makes no bones about awarding city contracts to people who pay his way." She lowered her voice an octave to emulate him: "'I figure those who contribute to my campaign are civic-minded citizens who want to support good government. Those are the sort of people I want to work with.'"

"A great way to solicit donations."

"We won't know how corrupt he really is until he leaves office and we see where he lands. He could mimic Mexican presidents and go into exile, or Illinois governors and go to prison."

"Business as usual."

Berkman studied him. "Doing some soul searching?"

"You know I sold that to the Devil years ago."

A cheer went up. The jukebox played "Auld Lang Syne." The revelers embraced, toasted, kissed. Gabriel bent and pressed his lips to Berkman's. Her perfume came to him with the creamy taste of her lipstick.

"Happy new year, Laura," he intoned.

She laughed. "That's the saddest 'happy new year' I ever heard."

"Sorry. Not much in a party mood."

"Pity. I had thought you might ask me to ride the elevator up with you tonight."

"I thought so too. But something pushed my down button."

"That doesn't sound like much fun. Well, we should at least have another drink."

"At least."

When Alice brought the next round she asked Laura how long she'd known Gabriel.

Berkman turned to him. "Nineteen years six months. Right, Carlo?"

"If you say so."

"My first month on the job. Cub reporter doing a series on North St. Louis drug dealing. Thought it would be enlivened if I could show the cops in action. They assigned Detective Gabriel to shepherd me around. And that he did."

"The cook's tour, no less. That's how we roll."

"I'm sensing a story here," Alice said.

Gabriel felt Laura pinching his leg. "You tell it since you thought it so damn funny."

"You have no idea how truly amusing it was. Third and final day out we thought to give the new girl a treat. Told her we were busting a dangerous drug kingpin. Showed her a mug shot of the villain—actually a photo of officer Marvin Davis dressed in a yellow pimp suit. We ride to a vacant flat on St. Louis Avenue and park in the side alley. I tell Roper to go up the back stairs. Mankewicz and I would go up the front. I turn to Laura and say, 'Geez, we're a man short. You wait here in the alley, and if the perp comes this way, you stall him till we get here.'

"Before she has time to protest we go busting ass into the building. A minute later we start yelling, 'There he goes! Out the back! Roper! Where's Roper?'

"Then we send Davis running down the alley in his yellow pimp suit. Of course we're all watching this from the second floor with the video cam. Laura starts tap-dancing and praying at the same time"—Gabriel clasped his hands together at his chest and did a brief shuffle—"wishing she was covering the garden club meeting. Want to see the tape?"

Alice gave them a round on the house. And another. Gabriel put Laura Berkman in a cab at one-thirty then went upstairs and right to bed. But he woke at six and couldn't get back to sleep.

- 15 -

Thursday morning, January 2nd. Gabriel had been at his desk for an hour catching up on paperwork when his cell phone buzzed. A woman's voice said:

"This is Marais, DNA lab. I was told to call you when we finished the mayor's rush job."

"And?"

"No go. Given the samples submitted, the swimmer and this Jonathan Stone are two different blokes."

"No question?"

"None."

He telephoned Ellen Cantrell, whose secretary answered, and learned she was in a meeting off premises. Gabriel sent a text message to her cell phone:

"Good news: No DNA match."

He sat looking at his desktop, eyes unfocused, for long minutes trying to organize his thoughts. The DNA results, coupled with the assertion of the testy Jesuit Father Mohan that Stone would never harm himself, suggested that the former professor was likely alive somewhere. That was supported by a lack of prior self-destructive tendencies and the serendipitous nature of his disappearance, coming about with the sudden dovetailing of trying personal circumstances. Then there was the purposeful abandonment of his wife's car, left behind as if to signal her of his estrangement. Further, apparently no one besides Gabriel and The Gecko—and possibly Father Mohan—knew of the potentially explosive research Stone had been conducting. And until certain parties did, Stone was in no danger from them. All this added up to a sobering conclusion: without any money trail or such to guide him, Gabriel was back where he started, nowhere.

He got out his notebook and flipped through it. Then he browsed the case file on his computer. Finally he grabbed his topcoat and walked to The Gecko's cubicle. He found him gazing at one of the computer screens glowing there. When he looked up, Gabriel said:

"Let's take a ride."

Still no sunshine, though the wind had eased. He aimed his unmarked black Dodge north on Union Boulevard.

"Nice car," said The Gecko.

"I'm told it can do a hundred and fifty."

"Flip on the siren and let's see."

Gabriel looked at him then back to the street ahead. "Gecko, my man, stick to the virtual world, where you're safe and warm."

Soon he turned right onto West Florissant Boulevard and asked, "Watch the Rose Bowl yesterday?"

They were talking football when he made a left into Bellefontaine Cemetery. Gabriel said: "Lewis and Clark— one of them's buried here."

"Likely Clark."

"Why you say that?"

"Lewis was shot dead in Mississippi."

"You a history buff?"

The Gecko shook his head. "Homicide enthusiast."

Unlike that along the city streets, the snow here— bounding plowed lanes curving between elaborate crypts— still lay pristine white. Gabriel stopped the car and killed the engine. "Let's walk."

The temperature readout on the Dodge had said thirty, but with the calm air it felt warmer. Yet The Gecko wore the flaps on his uniform-blue bomber's cap down over his ears. Gabriel walked with his cashmere topcoat open. After strolling in silence for fifty yards he said:

"Stone. He's still alive. At least the guy they found in the river ain't him."

"Is that the good news or the bad news?"

"For him, good; for me, bad."

"How'd Ellen Cantrell take it?"

"Not sure. She was tied up, so I texted her. But she's a hard one to read. Like a sponge: seems to absorb and make use of whatever is at hand, including men."

"O, baby, use me up!"

Gabriel stopped and turned toward him. "I realize that you know nothing about the actual details of Stone's secret files, since you claim you haven't read them. So let's talk hypothetically. Let's say she was banging the mayor and up to her tits in nefarious and illegal kickbacks and such and that her relationship with her husband—last in league power-rankings and a sociopolitical liability—had deteriorated to the backstabbing stage."

"Okay. But who was stabbing whom?"

"Very good, Gecko: who and whom, nominative case and objective case. Just read about it last night. And a good question. Along with, 'Who knew who was doing what to whom?'"

"Think she's capable of having him put away?"

"Don't be premature, Geck. Ellen Cantrell's living in a goldfish bowl that distorts everything on the outside. Worse, she doesn't realize it's actually a shark tank. Here's a crucial question: How reliable is Stone's information? He could be making it all up—the phone calls, the conversations, the emails, the hacked files. Or could he really assemble all that?"

"He could do it, no doubt. You have your cell phone in your pocket, lieutenant? Theoretically someone could be listening to our conversation through it."

"Even though it's off?"

"Absolutely. You can't begin to imagine what's possible these days. We can disable the GPS on your phone so they can't track you, but they could still be listening and watching and mining all sorts of info."

"How?"

"In two minutes I could install a program on your phone that would let me use its microphone as a listening device to hear any conversation within earshot. Or software that would allow me to monitor your calls and text messages. If you dial a particular number I'm interested in, I can be alerted automatically and secretly patched into the conversation."

"Shit."

"I can also send you a text message that, when you open it, will activate a GPS system that lets me track you step-by-step anywhere in the world. If you were a terrorist and I was the CIA, I could then put a missile in your ear."

"Okay, I hear you."

"Plus there's your computer: Easy enough for me to install a keystroke monitor on your laptop so I know every email, web address, and password you type. And I can access your whole web-browsing history. Put this together and I can follow trails to secret bank accounts, secret social-media personas, secret lovers, secret lives. Or I could simply plant a GPS tracking device in your car that let's me see what ATMs and girlfriends you visit even if you leave your phone at home. Tip of the iceberg. The technology changes every day."

"Any of this legal?"

"Most of it, I think, even without warrants. But technology's my thing, not law or ethics. Where does this leave you?"

"Up the creek, paddleless. This is one sorry-ass messy situation. Would have been a lot simpler if that had been Stone in the black bag—even though I've grown rather fond of the bastard.

"How rude of him to not have thrown himself into the mighty Mississippi."

"Yeah, so now I'm back to being an ineffective missing-persons cop tiptoeing through political minefields and no closer to finding the fleeing spouse—dead or alive. Plus, I need to ride this train to the end before I get my ticket punched."

They stopped at a large, Egyptianesque mausoleum guarded by a concrete sphinx on either side.

"Why are you telling me all this, Carlo?"

"I need some quick closure, my friend. The clock's ticking on this one. I've got to find him soon, wherever he might be. Otherwise I'll spend the rest of my professional days out here in North fucking St. Louis. After you discovered that first hidden cloud, you said you felt like you were being led on."

"Maybe, but maybe not on purpose. But people are people and leave traces of themselves—digital fingerprints—to guide you."

"Any idea where?"

The Gecko shrugged. "He's crafty. Likes wordplay and mystery and suspense, like a frustrated novelist. Maybe he left clues just as flourishes to amuse himself. Or maybe his wife has an idea."

"What do you mean?"

"She might be withholding some key info. Are you sure she wants you to find him? You sure she wants him back?"

Gabriel stared at him. "You're not as dumb as you look."

Gabriel's cell phone dinged in his coat pocket, and he pulled it out. "Speak of the devil. A text from Ellen Cantrell thanking me for the good news about the hubby and asking for his laptop back."

The Gecko looked at him and said, "Well, there you go."

- 16 -

Another evening home alone for Gabriel. Trying to stick to his low-carb diet, he poured himself some bourbon, made a salad, and fried a steak. As he ate he read about "tone" in his grammar book, about how the writer's attitude and vocabulary must suit the topic and the audience. After dinner he sat on the couch with his laptop and dove further into "The Eddy." It was like he was back in school, doing his homework.

By midnight he came to the last entry, dated nine a.m., Saturday, December 21, the morning Stone disappeared.

I say I distinguished myself at the faculty Christmas party yesterday—my last day at the university and perhaps my last as a teacher, given my behavior. I don't know what got into me. Well, yes I do: *in vino veritas* (via the two beers and shot of Jameson I had at lunch with Dadisi) and a crystalline sense of liberation—I've lost my job, my wife, my *raison d'etre*.

I had planned on skipping the event to avoid chitchat about my leaving. But the party was already going on when Dadisi and I returned, and he pulled me into the conference room.

I was sipping coffee and munching Christmas cookies when I heard the dinging of a spoon on glass. Everyone quieted and turned toward the punch bowl, where stood our fearless leader, Armand Betancourt.

He welcomed everyone, apologized for the lack of alcohol in the punch—ha ha—and announced: "This is my fifth Christmas party as department chairman and, I have learned, my last…"

Gasps. Mumbled condolences. Betancourt raised a hand to quiet the crowd.

"I've just learned that come July I will assume new duties as the Dean of the School of Arts and Sciences."

Cheers, a smattering of applause.

I muttered, "To succeed in life, you need two things: ignorance and confidence," just as the room quieted. Heads turned to me. I raised a hand as if in apology. "I didn't say that; Mark Twain did."

From across the room Betancourt glared at me. I waved at him.

"Don't worry, Armand. I'll keep your academic dishonesty secret—for the time being."

Stunned silence in the room.

"Enough, Stone. Let's keep this friendly."

"That's good coming from you, who a few hours ago threatened to sic campus police on me. Once again your totalitarian impulses kicking in."

"Is that all?"

"Just one other thing: Kiss my ass, you corrupt son of a bitch."

Another round of gasps.

"Not wise to slander with witnesses present, Stone."

"Not slander if I have proof, which I do—at least for the 'corrupt' part."

I saw Dadisi giving me a pleading look. He was right: guilt by association. Just because he was my office mate and we'd had lunch together, it could cost him with the vindictive Betancourt.

But Betancourt was right too: My exit speech was over-dramatic and uncivil. But how else to get people's attention these days?

All the world's a stage,
And all the men and women merely players;
They have their exits and their entrances,
And one man in his time plays many parts,…

I had already played three of Shakespeare's seven ages of man—the infant, the child, and the lover—all to no avail. Now perhaps time to portray the next: the soldier. So I bid everyone a "Merry Christmas!" and left.

Gabriel turned off his computer and gazed out over the darkened park. Stone's tone was not that of someone ready to take his own life. Rather, he sounded like someone ready to launch an attack. But Gabriel had no idea where or what sort.

§

Friday morning he was sitting on his couch in his robe drinking coffee and reading the *St. Louis Post-Dispatch* when his phone buzzed. No caller I.D. He answered anyway.

"Hey, Carlo, Ange. You still at home wasting taxpayer money, you lazy ass? Be downstairs in a half hour."

At eight-thirty Gabriel stood in his topcoat just inside the glass front doors of his building. He had stepped outside to wait and found that the air had turned bitter cold overnight, riding in on a brisk northerly wind, forcing him to retreat back inside.

Soon the mayor's black Lincoln Town Car pulled into the semicircular drive. Gabriel lifted his chin at the driver, who acknowledged him likewise, and dove into the back seat. There the mayor sat sipping coffee from a cardboard cup.

"Give us a minute, Lawrence."

The driver—Officer Monroe—got out, leaving the engine running, and stood on the curb with his collar up.

"Good thing the weather here's so crappy," said Cira. "Makes for affordable city living."

"That and the high crime rate. But we're doing our best, Mr. Mayor."

Cira laughed and slapped Gabriel's knee. "You know how to get along, Carlo. I still hear good things from the department. Everyone likes you. No bull."

"I try to get along, Ange."

Cira nodded, then frowned. "I know, I know. But I don't like the way this Jonathan Stone thing is dragging out."

"Like I said, we're doing our best. But you don't want any publicity, and without the public's help you know how tough it is to find someone—particularly if they're trying to dodge you. Either he's made himself hard to find—no money trail, no phone calls, no credit cards, no plane tickets, nothing—or maybe he's in the river after all."

Cira raised an eyebrow. "Is that what you think?"

Gabriel hesitated then said, "I don't know what to think. His wife thought him incapable of harming himself but may have changed her mind. He was under a lot of pressure, thought himself a failure."

"How do you know that?"

Now was the time for him to cover his ass.

"We found a journal of sorts on his laptop. Problem students, troubles with his boss, unable to finish his PhD dissertation, then he loses his job. And he had personal issues."

"Anything else?"

Gabriel looked through the windshield at Monroe, who had his back to the wind. "That was pretty much it for the journal," he said. "That and lots of research about educational issues and problems with the schools, which he seems bent on addressing."

"So you think he's still alive?"

"I do. And maybe a man on a mission."

The mayor sipped again at his coffee and looked away, gazing out the side window toward Forest Park.

"Let me be frank with you. This Stone could be a loose cannon. Maybe delusional to boot. An intellectual who doesn't understand politics or appreciate the real world. Who knows where his imagination has led him. He's a nobody, but that doesn't mean he couldn't cause problems. If he files for divorce and makes accusations—no matter how wrongheaded—all that is public. With that comes questions and putting me on the defensive with Milton Jackson Holmes breathing down my neck in the primary.

Doesn't make any difference if it's all bullshit. It could still cost me votes."

Gabriel waited.

"Track him down and shut him up. Do what's necessary. I wouldn't want to have to bring anyone else in on this." He turned back and laid a gloved hand on Gabriel's coat sleeve. "But when you find him don't take any chances. He might be feeling desperate. He could be armed. You understand? We need to dissuade him in whatever way from doing anything stupid. We both have a lot riding on this."

Gabriel stared at the mayor but Cira avoided his eyes, sipping at his coffee and looking again out the side window toward the park. "You know, Carlo, it might have been better for all of us if that had been him in river."

When he turned back their eyes met. Gabriel had seen that gaze before, and even after thirty years it still chilled him. He opened the door and got out without another word. He stood on the sidewalk watching Cira's limo pull away and turn south, watched it until it disappeared from view. Then he turned and went back inside.

§

Later that morning Gabriel drove back to the SLU campus. The clock was indeed ticking. The mayor had put pressure on him. Now he would funnel it along in hopes of finding a leak.

He parked beside Saint Francis Xavier College Church across the street from Jesuit Hall, where he had recently interviewed Father Mohan. The church was a white-stone structure with soaring steeple—Gothic, thought Gabriel, though he wasn't sure. Ornate—that he was certain of. The sort of sanctuary only Catholics would build. Gabriel locked his cellphone in the glove box and stepped out into the cold.

As he walked up the front steps toward the tall wooden doors he remembered walking down those steps with Janet on his arm in her wedding dress. What sort of optimism had compelled him to make that leap? He really couldn't recall and didn't want to try.

He found Father Mohan waiting for him in the vestibule, this time wearing a black cassock. They did not shake hands.

"You surprise me, Mr. Gabriel," the priest said by way of greeting. "I didn't think you'd take me up on my offer to hear your confession so soon."

"God moves in mysterious ways."

Inside the massive vaulted church the only other person was a thin, gray-haired man working an electric floor-polisher over the wood parquet. The sanctuary was but softly lit, minimal light coming from the high, stained-glass windows. The ornate altar, which mimicked the church's façade, glowed yellow.

Gabriel followed Mohan to one of the beige-curtained confessionals built along the north wall where, as a SLU criminal justice student, he gave his confession weekly.

Inside as he knelt, the smell of the wood, the darkness, the quiet put him back as an undergrad trying to figure it all out, trying to get it right and do the right thing. He sensed a shadow of Mohan behind the wooden screen.

"Bless me, Father, for I have sinned. Since my last confession it's been twenty, maybe twenty-five years."

"Close enough. Any mortal sins in the past three

decades?"

"A couple of the Ten Commandments, Father: Thou shalt not kill—though in the line of duty. Thou shalt not commit adultery on several occasions. I stole, coveted my neighbor's wife, and blasphemed. I got divorced. On the upside, I always honored my father and mother."

"Thank God for that."

Gabriel looked up again to the wooden screen that separated the two men. "Want to hear some venial sins?"

"Do we have time?"

"Actually, there's something more important I want to talk about and why I'm here: Jonathan Stone."

"In hopes of delivering a message à la Gabriel the Archangel? Then why not just call me?"

"To protect you, Father. And me."

"From what?"

"The forces of evil. At least as Stone saw them."

"You mean you think he's dead?"

"A grammatical error. I think he's still alive. No DNA match on a man we pulled from the river. But I'm concerned that his days may be numbered."

"How's that?"

"The mayor asked me to kill him. Of course, not in so many words. But you don't need too many words to get that kind of meaning across. And soon I may not be the only one hunting him."

After a pause Mohan asked, "Can we back up here? Mayor Angelo Cira asked you to murder Jonathan Stone?"

"This morning. Over coffee in the back seat of his limo. Like I said, it's not that he came right out and said it, but it's what I read between the lines and in his eyes. Bottom line is he thinks things would be nicer and easier without Stone running around mucking them up."

He heard the rustling of the cassock as Mohan shifted in his seat.

"Additional back story," Gabriel continued. "I suspect Stone told you about his job troubles and his straying wife. But there's more, which you may or may not know. He learned that she's involved with the mayor not only sexually but also in a multimillion-dollar kickback scheme related to Stadium Towne. My electronic-discovery geek was able to find documentation in files Stone thought he had hidden in an online storage box. We suspect that the mayor's people have by now found those same files. Which is why he wants Stone dealt with."

There was a longer silence. Finally Mohan spoke, his voice low. "Tell me why, lieutenant, would the mayor think you would commit murder for him?"

Gabriel looked down at his hands and saw in the dim light that they were folded as if in prayer. He separated them.

"I forgot to mention another mortal sin, Father: bearing false witness. Angelo Cira and I were young cops together. Went through the academy and worked side by side. Once, Cira shot an unarmed suspect and needed some cover. I provided it. So you might say there's an expectation that I perform as a team player. There's a bond."

"Of a certain sort."

"But I know Angelo Cira and know that for him loyalty is a one-way street. He worships but one God: Angelo Cira. Not that that distinguishes him from other politicians. The rest of us are disposable if we get in his way, and Jonathan

Stone could end up being a major roadblock. Anything he might have told you about his plans might help me find him."

"In order to kill him?"

Gabriel brought his hands to his face, rubbing his eyes. "Okay. So I'm somewhat corruptible, Father. Doesn't follow that I'm capable of cold-blooded murder. I hate this case. Thought it would be easy. Track down this egghead and get back in the hierarchy. Get my old job back. But then I start stepping in all this other shit—sorry. Incompetent schools, drugged-out parents, discouraged students. Faithless wives, dirty politicians, surly Jesuits. I'm fed up."

"That's it, get it off your chest."

"All I want to do is wrap this up and wash my hands of it. I figure if I can find Stone—given he's not in the river, which might still be a possibility. If I can find him I can lay out what he's gotten himself into and persuade him to back off. I can put him on ice and go to Cira to reassure him. Ange trusts me."

"In other words, sweep everything under the carpet."

"In other words, save the poor bastard's life while keeping the mayor happy and keeping my job. Cira's already threatened to hand this off to someone else if I don't deliver, likely someone not as sensitive to Stone's long-term well-being. Besides, I don't think the mayor really wants me to kill him. Just keep him quiet."

"You might not find that so easy. You don't know Jonathan Stone."

"I think I do. You may have heard his confession, but I read most all of it last night, some two hundred pages. His passion isn't politics, Father. It's participles and prepositions.

And seeing kids get a fair shake. Yeah, he's angered and humiliated by his wife's adultery and feeling vindictive right now. But he's also keen on acting from the better parts of himself, not from spite."

After a beat Mohan said, "That would seem to suggest his dedication to exposing the corruption he's discovered."

"I think he could live with a minor sin of omission, Father."

"He who stands idly by is just as guilty as he who holds the knife."

"But in this case there's no knife, no bloodshed. Just a little money under the table. That is, business as usual. Which is not likely to change, no matter what Stone does or who's mayor. Hardly something worth sacrificing his life for, a life that could profit others if focused on the things that really matter to him. Besides, he couldn't pull it off by himself. Cira's no doubt already covering his tracks. Probably nothing any of us can do about it short of exorcising City Hall."

"I'd like a shot at that."

"In the meantime, Father, don't you commit a sin of omission by not helping me find and persuade Stone to get on the right course to save himself. If you know something and can't tell me, at least let him know what I'm up to and why. Let him choose."

Gabriel stared at the wooden screen where he sensed Mohan sitting stock-still. At last the priest spoke. "Perhaps I can help you, lieutenant, with a suggestion."

"What's that?"

"Pray to Saint Anthony, patron of missing persons."

Gabriel laughed. "'Something's lost and can't be found/

Please, St. Anthony, look around.' You are a pip, Father. Give me my penance, and I'll get the hell out of here."

- 17 -

Back home that evening Gabriel dipped once again into "The Eddy" hoping to discover something that might help him find Stone. That afternoon he had tried meditating on it in the sauna at the Y. Afterward he spent some time at the North Patrol Division bouncing ideas off The Gecko to no good effect. Then he sat in his office perusing *English Grammar for Idiots*, hidden inside a binder on Missing Persons Procedure, as if searching for clues as to how Stone's mind might have been altered by teaching remedial grammar. It certainly made Gabriel more aware of the nuances in speech and what others, such as Father Mohan, might really intend—though the priest was hardly subtle. Maybe it had made Stone more aware of the subtext in his wife's pronouncements.

Paging through the document he came upon some salacious bits he had only skimmed the previous night. He backed up and started reading in earnest.

It was there from the beginning. She had come home with me after our Monday evening creative writing seminar, where we had met the previous week. I opened a bottle of wine. As we toasted and drank I noticed a bit of lace peeking out atop her silky blouse. I touched her there, just grazing the backs of my fingers along the lace, and said, "This looks nice."

"Would you like to see it?"

"Of course."

She set down her drink, discarded her blouse and slid her blue jeans down over her hips to reveal ivory-colored bustier, bikini and stockings.

"You like?"

I ran a thumb up the outside of her thigh. "I like very much."

We exhausted ourselves and, hours later, fell asleep in each other's arms. When I woke the next morning she was gone.

Over time our repertoire grew. Once she arrived with silk ribbons for me to bind her. Another time with beads. Yet another with ointments and vibrators of various sizes.

Soon we both recognized something different transpiring, which made previous sexual encounters seem insipid by comparison. We'd meet at my apartment after a day spent living asensually, in the intellect, in sterile classrooms and libraries. We'd spend hours tasting and exploring each other—nothing was forbidden, no want taboo, nothing that could not be requested and fulfilled. We soon learned that by limiting ourselves to one weekly liaison, we could intensify that pleasure—pleasure that would deliver me somewhere entirely away from my mind, to a utopia that exceeded my imagination. I have never used hard drugs, but I think I got a glimpse of the euphoria that heroin users claim.

There was little laughter between us at these times. We entered our candlelit cathedral with solemnity to perform our sacred rites—the seriousness and sense of purpose appropriate as we moved nearer to nature, nearer to God. And only recently, in the last year, has that vision of heaven dimmed.

Gabriel stroked his mustache wondering if The Gecko had read this part and fired his imagination re: Ellen Cantrell. It gave Gabriel pause as well—and not just because of the erotic distance between Ellen Cantrell and his own ex-wife. And not because the Stone-Cantrell relationship was that unusual—he had known transcendent moments himself, if not with Janet and if not with the intensity felt by the hypersensitive Stone. But it revealed a cosmic connection between Stone and his wife. Its loss—having Paradise stolen from him—would likely produce profound effects. Maybe even to the extent that he might be a danger to himself or others. Gabriel had seen it happen before, far too many times. He thought of Leslie Hardaway, the strangled honor student, and her distraught former lover, a young man who had lost the only beautiful thing he had ever known.

§

Saturday morning Gabriel woke to find an email from The Gecko: "Call me as arranged." He smiled. After a cup of coffee he found the safe number The Gecko had given him, dressed in sweats, and took the elevator to the lobby commons. There he went to the building's meeting room and called from the fax machine. He heard The Gecko answer and said:

"Secret agent double-o-sixty-nine?"

"This is serious."

"Okay, okay. What's up?"

"Staying on top of the Stone thing like you said. Since I returned his laptop to his wife I've been monitoring things. I don't know what this means, if it's good or bad, whether it means Stone's alive or whether—"

"Spit it out, Gecko."

"His two cloud storage accounts where he kept his research, both have been emptied. Either he did it or 'they' did it."

"'They' being, in your estimation…?"

"It could be the Cyber Crime Unit at headquarters. If I could find this stuff, they certainly could. But if I were the party involved, a party interested in keeping a lid on things, I'd be more inclined to give the job to a private supplier. Or to a knowledgeable relative or confidant. Maybe hand it off to someone who's got a stake in burying it."

"Like the big-money boys at Stadium Towne."

"Since I didn't read the files, I have no idea what you're talking about, but it just as well could have been Stone who deleted it."

"Despite it happening the day after Ellen Cantrell again got her hands on his computer and I had alerted Cira to the existence of a journal? Unlikely. Stone was obsessing over his research for months. Why delete it now?"

After a pause The Gecko said, "A couple possible reasons: One, he discovered he'd been hacked into and moved it to a safer place. Two, someone was holding a gun to his head."

"Or he thought they were."

"Meaning?"

"You'd rather not know, believe me."

Gabriel realized that both of The Gecko's scenarios could have derived from Gabriel's confession with Father Mohan, who may have tipped Stone off as he had been asked to do. The first scenario was bad, at least for Gabriel's purposes: a Jonathan Stone going to ground, digging in for a protracted battle against the mayor et al.; the second scenario, good: a Jonathan Stone intimidated into silence by the thought of the mayor's gunman, Gabriel, being on his tail with instructions to silence him by whatever means.

"You back up the files?"

"No way," The Gecko said. "Just the two flash drives I gave you. See no evil, hear no evil, download no evil."

"Okay. Thanks. I'll think on it."

But Gabriel didn't know what to think.

However, he had noted one thing. The Gecko had said, "If I *were* the party involved," not "If I *was* the party involved." That is, he used the subjunctive mood to express something contrary to fact, improbable, or doubtful, according to *English Grammar for Idiots*. Similarly, Gabriel had to start thinking as if he were a distraught English professor. Being a detective, he was learning, meant living in the subjunctive.

- 18 -

Back upstairs, he finished his coffee and watched the traffic on Skinker, considering what his next move should be. Pressuring Father Mohan may have stirred things up, but he figured it was time to see what a little pressure on Ellen Cantrell would do. He dialed her cell phone and asked to see her. She told him to come by her place in an hour, sounding like she'd just gotten up or hadn't slept.

He dressed for success in black blazer with silk tie and motored across the park to grab breakfast at one of his favorite cafés on its east side. Afterward, when Gabriel tried to pay for his omelet, the owner, who manned the cash register, wouldn't allow it.

"Next time you pay, Carlo."

"You said that last time, Max. And the time before."

"Don't stay away so long," Max said with a laugh. "Then I won't forget what I say." Gabriel knew it wasn't his sparkling personality that Max liked, but rather the knowledge that a friend on the force was a good thing to have, like when Max's soft-minded son-in-law got caught up in a drug bust.

"Can't stay away from your breakfasts for too long," Gabriel said and then turned up the collar on his overcoat and pushed out the door onto the street. The Arctic wind still blew, stinging his face. He pulled on his gloves and looked at his watch. He was right on time.

He walked up Laclede Avenue to Kingshighway Boulevard and the ABC condominiums—an appropriate address for an English teacher. Actually the ABCDs, the names chiseled into the pediments above the four entrances: Aberdeen, Bellevue, Colchester, and Devonshire. A hundred years after construction they were still a desirable place to live and well beyond an honest cop's pay.

He got buzzed into the Devonshire, took the elevator to the sixth floor—the penthouse—found the apartment on the right, and knocked.

Despite it being over an hour since they talked, Ellen Cantrell came to the door in an aquamarine bathrobe. She didn't look all that great without makeup—circles under her eyes, the beginnings of crow's feet at the corners, and, worse, a general sense of fatigue that clung to her like cheap perfume. She let him in without a word, and he followed her to the kitchen.

The apartment was tastefully decorated. Older, elegant things. Red brocade wallpaper in the vestibule, French-looking chairs and sofa glimpsed as he passed the living room, landscape paintings or reproductions—Impressionist?—on the walls. Money can buy most anything, including taste and interior decorators. He could not see Ellen Cantrell perusing Martha Stewart magazines to get ideas.

He sat at the counter as she stood across from him pouring two cups from what appeared to be an industrial-strength coffeemaker. When she set his cup on the counter, her hand shook. She didn't ask if he wanted sugar or cream.

"Thanks for seeing me on short notice," he said.

"You said you didn't want to talk on the phone."

"Just wanted to make sure there was no miscommunication."

She picked up her cup and held it between her hands as if they were cold—or as if she needed to occupy or steady them. "What is it you have to communicate?"

"I was hoping *you* might have something to communicate to help *me* find your husband."

She stared at him. "You mean you have nothing new to tell me?" She set her coffee cup down carefully, impatience creeping into her voice. "I've already *communicated* to you everything I can."

He sipped his coffee and waited a beat. Then, "There is something new. Something that raises the stakes. Something that suggests some urgency."

"What?" She straightened.

"Your husband's life may be at risk."

"What are you talking about? First you tell me he's drowned, then he's alive, and now he's in danger."

Gabriel ran his fingers along the rim of his cup trying to get the language right in his mind.

"I know why I was chosen for this assignment, Ms. Cantrell. Angelo Cira and I go back thirty years. He trusts me. He values my discretion. I want you to trust me as well. So I will give you my pledge: Nothing we say to each other in the next ten minutes will leave this room by my doing. And I hope not by yours." Ellen nodded and brushed the hair off her forehead. Gabriel went on, "What did you do with your husband's laptop once it was returned to you two days ago?"

"An officer from headquarters came for it."

"Did he say why?"

She shrugged. "No, and I didn't ask. I figured it was evidence or something."

"Did you know what secrets it contained?"

"Secrets? Jonathan isn't the type of man to have secrets."

"You know nothing about his Cloud IX accounts?"

"I have no idea what you're talking about."

He nodded as if considering her words. "Okay. I didn't think so." He waited. Took another long drink of coffee.

"Are you going to tell me what this is all about?"

He set his cup down. "Did you know your husband had stopped working on his dissertation? That he was instead chronicling the events that led to his getting sacked at the university. That he's spent months gathering incriminating evidence against his boss and others in what he termed 'educational malpractice.' That he was writing about his marital problems and about you and … well…."

Her eyes went wide and her mouth dropped open in an unspoken, *Oh*. Gabriel held her gaze and continued. "Marital issues aside, the most important thing at this point is what he wrote about ongoing corruption at City Hall, including your involvement in payoffs and kickbacks on the Stadium Towne project."

"What?" Her body stiffened like she had just been slapped.

"Apparently he felt humiliated and vindictive and so put to use his considerable writing and computer skills to dig into things he had no legal right to—including your email and bank accounts. Now, however, since you gave his laptop to headquarters and, by extension, to Angelo, all that information has been deleted from his online cloud accounts."

She opened her mouth to speak, but he held up his hand to silence her.

"Now, it could be coincidence. Your husband may have come to his senses and trashed the stuff himself, seeing what damage it could do to you, the mayor, and others. But coincidence just doesn't smell right in this case since the files—which have existed in some form for months—vanished within forty-eight hours of the downtown boys getting theirs hands on his computer."

She went into herself. Gabriel sensed the walls going up. He leaned forward and pressed on.

"You're not naïve, Ms. Cantrell. You know they play hardball downtown when they want to shut somebody up. Usually they're happy enough simply to sully someone's reputation, ruin him financially, or send him to prison. Not that difficult when you have the police, the judges, the media, and the mob on your side. But your husband may feel he has little left to lose at his point and thus might be hard to silence by traditional means. I'm keen on finding him and talking some sense into him. Unlike some, I'm keen on keeping him alive."

Cantrell stared at the marble countertop shaking her head. "I can't believe it." When she looked up her bottom lip quivered if just for an instant. "You must be wrong."

"You know better than I what you revealed to Jonathan and what he might have discovered on his own—and the potential political and legal damage that could result if he made that information public. So I'm also hoping you can give me a clue, anything that might help me find him before something happens. Before the next body we pull out of the river really is your husband's." He waited for that to sink in.

"Think about where he might be hiding," he continued. "Any place you vacationed together? Any friends he might have communicated with? We checked the people he had emailed and talked with recently, but no dice. What about cousins, classmates, prior girlfriends?"

She bit her lip. "We've been together since college. There's no one else … We never traveled much. First there was grad school. Then he was always teaching, and I was working round-the-clock. But Jonathan didn't seem to mind. He had his books—that's where he traveled. And his dissertation—Mark Twain, Hannibal, and all that … I just don't know.…"

With that she seemed to pull even further into herself. He got up and let himself out without a word, leaving her leaning against the kitchen counter, staring off into space. It was a wasted conversation in that she gave him nothing new, but he did take away something from the meeting: Laura Berkman and Jonathan Stone were probably right— Ellen Cantrell didn't seem all that bright. How people like her got into positions of power he'd never know. Okay, he did know, but that didn't mean he liked it.

Despite his plea for confidentiality, he figured she'd panic and immediately call the mayor. Gabriel couldn't control what Ellen Cantrell did, so he'd just have to wait and see what happened next on that front. Besides, it wouldn't make any difference—Angelo would just think Gabriel was doing his job, scaring her, blowing smoke up her ass to get her to divulge whatever information she might be guarding. The mayor would see that the lieutenant was on the job, following his directive to do whatever necessary to find Stone. But Cantrell would eventually have to decide who to trust to keep her husband alive.

Unless, of course, that's not what she wanted.

- 19 -

From the the Cantrell's apartment Gabriel walked two blocks north to Straub's grocery. Though just midday, he decided to get something for later that evening, figuring to chill again on a Saturday night. If he got bored and restless he could always call Laura Berkman—or Jasmine. But that seemed unlikely. He needed to bear down on finding Stone. It had been two weeks. Something had to break.

With a piece of sea bass, some Mexican asparagus, and a bottle of white Bordeaux in a shopping bag, he walked back to his car and drove west across the park. After putting away the groceries, he punched the remote, and another bowl game came into focus on the TV. What with all the educational stuff floating around the case—schools, college sports, teachers, grammar lessons, final grades, and Stone's dissertation—he felt like he was on semester break with everyone else. Might as well have a couple of beers to complete the mood. It was still early, but he popped a cold one and poured out a pile of nuts in a bowl, then muted the TV and settled in on the couch. He opened his laptop and plugged in the first flash drive that The Gecko had given him.

"The Masks of Mark Twain: Mis-identification, Subterfuge and Disappearance as a River to Truth," Gabriel read aloud. He might need more than a couple of beers to get through this, he thought.

He scanned the Table of Contents, where he found chapters on a number of Twain's works. Gabriel remembered reading *Adventures of Huckleberry Finn* in high school, if recalling few of its details. As a boy he'd seen movie versions of *The Prince and the Pauper* and *A Connecticut Yankee in King Arthur's Court*, both also covered here. There was a chapter on *Pudd'nhead Wilson*—that one he didn't know. He clicked to it and read.

As with *The Prince and the Pauper*, Twain's undervalued *Pudd'nhead Wilson* (elevated by its mystery, grim humor, and penetrating portrayal of the antebellum South), depicts two boys of the same age whose identities are switched—in this case one a privileged white aristocrat, the other a "black" slave under the existing law thanks to his 1/32 of African blood. As with other works of Twain analyzed here, this tale's roots can be traced to his fanciful Hannibal childhood with its class and racial complexities, yearnings for transformation, and the young Samuel Clemens' obsession with role-playing and disguise….

Gabriel shrugged. He scrolled back up to *Connecticut Yankee* and read of Hank Morgan, a 19th century Hartford resident who, after a blow to the head, finds himself transported to medieval England where he is mistaken for a knight. Gabriel skimmed the chapter, finding nothing in the tale—or what Stone had to say about it—that seemed of any help. On to *Huckleberry Finn*.

> Key to Huckleberry's transformation—and his ultimate subversion of accepted "wisdom" regarding slavery—is his compulsion to escape his own domestic chains, i.e., his enforced solitude and his father's drunken violence. During his father's absence he escapes, devising the elaborate staging of his own death, and sets off down the Mississippi.

Gabriel looked up, gazing at the gray afternoon outside and the monochromatic park with its black-trunked trees and ashen snow below a leaden sky. He was thinking of Jonathan Stone. He recalled reading in "The Eddy" Stone's confession of his soiled marital life, his humiliation by his wife's unfaithfulness, her boozy braggadocio, and his own domestic chains. Good Catholic boy that he was, for whom divorce was not an option, he felt trapped in an unholy alliance with a woman whom he had found to be immoral, corrupt, and criminal.

Gabriel vaguely recalled that Huck had taken off down river while others had presumed him dead, but forgot exactly how he did it. Now he was curious.

On a website that catalogued old books now in the public domain he found an 1885 Charles L. Webster and Company edition. The title page read, "Adventures of Huckleberry Finn (Tom Sawyer's Comrade). By Mark Twain. With one hundred and seventy-four illustrations." In the contents he located what seemed a likely spot for his search:

"CHAPTER VII. Laying for Him.—Locked in the

Cabin.—Sinking the Body.—Resting."

There Gabriel found Huck's serendipitous escape plan: While hunting in the woods he came upon and shot a wild pig. He used its blood to stage a murder scene at his father's cabin, breaking in the door with an axe, smearing the axe with blood, and sticking on some of his own hair for good measure. Then he dragged a sack of rocks to the river to simulate a body being disposed of there and left clues to indicate a robbery. Now all he had to do was disappear, and he was free.

> It was about dark now; so I dropped the canoe down the river under some willows that hung over the bank, and waited for the moon to rise. I made fast to a willow; then I took a bite to eat, and by and by laid down in the canoe to smoke a pipe and lay out a plan. I says to myself, they'll follow the track of that sackful of rocks to the shore and then drag the river for me. And they'll follow that meal track to the lake and go browsing down the creek that leads out of it to find the robbers that killed me and took the things. They won't ever hunt the river for anything but my dead carcass. They'll soon get tired of that, and won't bother no more about me.

Gabriel sipped at his beer. Maybe that's what Stone wanted: for people to think he was dead, for no one to bother any more about him. But Gabriel wanted something too, and the only way to get it was to find Stone—dead or alive.

- 20 -

Next morning the valet had brought his Dodge up from the garage and had it waiting at the curb. Gabriel stepped to it through snow flurries coming in horizontally. He threw his bag in the trunk and slipped behind the wheel.

He drove west on the Parkway, north on the Inner Belt, west on Interstate 70. After he crossed the Missouri River at St. Charles he soon headed north on Missouri 79, which paralleled the Mississippi. He could have traveled quicker going up the newer four-lane highway. But he wanted to stay on the flood plain and pass through the hilly river towns like Clarksville and Louisiana where the riverboats piloted by a young Sam Clemens had put in. If he was going to find Stone—he was now convinced—he had to think not only as if he *were* a professor but also as if he *were* Mark Twain. His target was doing the same, he gauged and hoped, apparently channeling his master.

Gabriel sensed a solid beauty in the countryside's somber winter palette: muted grays and browns—the sky, the hills, the river, the fields, now dusted with the falling snow. He stopped at Clarksville where stood one of a series of dams that now tamed the upper Mississippi, making it more a series of lakes than the fierce and capricious force Twain wrote about in *Life on the Mississippi*.

In a diner on a low hill overlooking the dam he got eggs and bacon and ongoing chatter from a middle-aged black waitress eager, apparently, to talk to one of her own people for a change.

"You here for the eagles?"

"What eagles?"

She tilted her head toward the wide windows overlooking the river. "The bald eagles. Only reason people come in winter, watch the eagles catch fish."

He studied the river, pocked with ice, and soon saw a great black bird with a white head glide down and snatch a fish from the waters with its talons. Could he swoop in and find Professor Stone with the same efficiency? He didn't know, but he was damn sure gonna try.

Back outside, Gabriel had to brush a thin blanket of snow from the Charger's rear window before getting back on the road. As it wound it's way north, the dark, glistening highway twisted through hills covered with bare black trees and across beige valleys where he spied wild turkeys feeding in shorn cornfields. The road rose to cliffs from which he glimpsed the river and, beyond it, Illinois bottomland with bordering limestone bluffs.

He passed the sign—Hannibal, population 17,757—and found himself on Mark Twain Drive. The snow let up as he cruised around town. Clemens Avenue. A billboard advertising the Injun Joe Campground. Signs for the Mark Twain Dinette, The Becky Thatcher Restaurant, and Mrs. Clemens Antiques & Ice Cream. He found Tom Sawyer's Fence and the Mark Twain Boyhood Home and Museum. There was also a Mark Twain Cave, Mark Twain Hotel

Apartments ("affordable housing for senior citizens"), Mark Twain High School, Middle School and Elementary School, and Mark Twain Behavioral Health. At least they didn't name it for Huck Finn.

He parked downtown at the marina, and walked to the Mark Twain Statue and then to the river's edge. The old two-lane bridge he remembered from a childhood school trip was gone, and the river sped by dark and frightening, chunks of ice bobbing on its surface. He thought again of the jumper from Eads Bridge and the body in the morgue with its face sliced off. With a shiver, he moved back to his car.

He drove up Broadway and found the Holy Family Church. Sunday Mass was likely finished, according to a sign listing weekly services and the Friday night bingo. Nearby a man in a hooded red parka tossed salt on newly swept sidewalks.

Gabriel killed the engine on the Dodge and asked the man where he might find the priest.

"Father Salas?" The man glanced at his watch. "Depends on what time's kickoff. You'll most likely find him watching the game," he said, directing him to a tavern in a downtown hotel.

At the hotel restaurant the priest was easy to spot given the handyman's description. He was the only patron at the bar wearing a Dallas Cowboys jersey. A wildcard playoff game was under way.

"Father Salas?"

He turned from the TV, a stein of beer, and some nachos. He was a young man, maybe thirty, bespectacled, paunchy, and Mexican. "Yes?"

"May I have a word with you about an official police matter?"

The priest turned back to the screen for an instant then held his thumb and forefinger a millimeter apart. "Just a minute," he said with a trace of accent. "Till the quarter."

When a commercial appeared, Salas wiped his lips on a paper napkin and walked over to Gabriel, who had taken a seat at a table near the door. He showed the priest his badge and a photo of Jonathan Stone.

"I was wondering, Father, if you've seen this man?"

Salas took the photo and studied it. "Is he wanted by the police?"

"In a way. A missing person. We're trying to find him before he can harm himself." He left it at that.

"Maybe. Last week. At Tuesday morning Mass. But I'm not sure. Unusual to see a young man on weekdays. He sat in back. Then he came forward to take the Eucharist."

"And this morning?"

"I don't recall seeing him."

"Confession?"

The priest shook his head. "Nope."

Gabriel put his tongue in his cheek, thinking.

The priest turned to gaze at the TV, where the teams were lining up. "Anything else, detective?"

"Go Cowboys!" Gabriel cheered. Salas gave him a high five and hurried back to his barstool, and Gabriel made his way back out into the cold.

If Father Salas had in fact seen Jonathan Stone, then Father Mohan was right and Stone was still alive—or at least he was five days ago. And maybe Gabriel himself was right; perhaps he'd picked up Stone's trail.

§

The Hannibal Police Department was also on Broadway. It was a newer, boxy, two-story redbrick building. Once inside, Gabriel identified himself to the officer at the reception desk. She told him to have a seat and made a call. Soon another uniformed officer—thirtyish, crewcut, muscles bulging beneath his blue shirt—approached and held out his hand to shake. Smedstead, his nametag read, said he'd been working on the request Gabriel had called in, and they headed down the hall to an office with four desks, computer monitors and keyboards on each.

"Pretty slow today. Vehicles sliding into ditches. Nothing as exciting as a missing person."

"You don't know the half of it," said Gabriel as he sat.

"Hereabouts," said Smedstead as he manipulated the keyboard, "it's property crimes and hillbilly heroin—methamphetamine. Domestic disputes. Giving directions to tourists—in summer I'm on bicycle patrol downtown.

"There we are. Nothing showing on your man at the hotels—we got only five and a handful of B & Bs. Emailed them the photo you sent. Negative so far. Doesn't mean a night clerk didn't check him in under a different name. And he could have rented a room somewhere."

"I just talked with Father Salas from Holy Family. Said he may have seen him at Mass last Tuesday."

"Could have moved on by now. Why you think he'd come here?"

"Some noodling and a hunch. He's a professor doing research on Twain and his Hannibal boyhood. Seemed possible he might want to soak up some local atmosphere while he finished writing it."

"Local atmosphere we got. Nothing on his credit cards?"

Gabriel shrugged. "That's what I don't get. What he's living on? Where'd he get the cash? What he's using for transportation?"

"Must have been planning it, squirreling away some money."

"Maybe. Lots of guys keep slush funds, if only to buy a new set of golf clubs when the wife wants a dining-room set."

Smedstead turned to him, thinking. "Or a new deer rifle…."

"Anyway I thought I might ask around, flash the photo."

"Come with me. Less explaining to do."

Smedstead was proud of his new patrol car, a traditional black-and-white with "Hannibal Police Home of Mark Twain" painted on the sides and equipped with all the computerized bells and whistles. He demonstrated an automatic digital camera that started as soon as you flipped on the flashers.

They tried a couple bars—the football game now in overtime—without good result and moved on to the Mark Twain Family Restaurant.

Business there was slow on a snowy Sunday. Three waitresses, all in their twenties, gathered round and gawked at Stone's photo. A blonde elbowed the brunette next to her.

"That's him! But without the beard. The one you wanted to shag."

The brunette slapped the blonde's shoulder. "I did not say that! Just said he was cute."

"It was implied." The blonde—Marcella, said her

nametag—put her hands to her hips and gyrated, bringing laughter from the others.

Gabriel asked the brunette, "Josie, when did you first experience this mad desire?"

She couldn't stop giggling. Finally she managed to say, "When was it he came in? Suzanne was on too, so it must have been Friday."

"What time?'

"Dinner time. Maybe six."

"How was he dressed?"

"Sharp. Preppy, like a college boy. Corduroy jacket. Turtleneck."

"Anything else?"

"Left a three dollar tip for a ten dollar dinner."

"Notice what he was driving—or if he was?"

Neither had.

"And I assume he was alone."

"Yep. Just sat there reading."

"Reading what?'

"Well…" Josie paused, all eyes on her. She milked the moment then said: "When I brought him his plate—fried catfish dinner—and he closed the book, I saw that it was a grammar book. That's when I figured he was a teacher."

"Right you are."

"Did he run off with a student?"

"You wish!" said Marcella.

"He armed and dangerous?"

"I think you're safe," said Gabriel, grinning.

"Darn."

Smedstead added, "Give us a call, girls, if you see him again." Back behind the wheel of the patrol car he said,

"Seems like he's still around. We'll find him sooner or later."

"Has to be sooner."

"Could put his picture in the *Courier-Post*."

"Let me think on that."

Smedstead edged the car from the curb. "That's where Mark Twain first worked, setting type at the *Missouri Courier*."

"He's everywhere here, isn't he?"

Smedstead shrugged. "It's all we got."

- 21 -

Sunday night in Hannibal started early. By five-thirty the streets were dark, and everything had closed except for a few taverns. Gabriel got a room downtown in a newer hotel and called The Gecko's safe number from his room phone.

"Area code five-seven-three—where the hell's that?" he asked Gabriel.

"Stone's alive. At least he was last Friday."

"You tell Ellen Cantrell?"

"Just texted her to that effect. Anything new on your end?"

"Nothing. Still no credit card action."

"Damn. Looks like more footwork. Luckily there aren't too many places to put your feet up around here."

"Jeez, area code five-seven-three covers half the fricking state. Here we are, the Hannibal Huck Finn Inn on Mark Twain Drive."

"You can't escape him."

"Good luck getting back. More snow coming in tomorrow."

"I already feel stranded. Nothing here but woods, cornfields and the river."

After they hung up, Gabriel got out his laptop. First

he checked his email. Nothing pertinent. Then back to Stone's dissertation, skimming it and thinking on pressing matters—such as Stone's whereabouts—without good result. Then he returned to *Huckleberry Finn*.

He followed Huck to Jackson's Island, where he surprises the runaway slave, Jim, who, like others in Hannibal, thought Huck murdered and dumped in the Mississippi.

> "Doan' hurt me—don't! I hain't ever done no harm to a ghos'. I alwuz liked dead people, en done all I could for 'em. You go en git in de river agin, whah you b'longs, en doan' do nuffn to Ole Jim, 'at 'uz awluz yo' fren'."

Perhaps best for Ole Carlo, too, if Stone would go back into the river where he belonged—or at least where the mayor would have him reside.

Huck went on to disabuse Jim of the idea that he was dead.

> "Well, I warn't long making him understand I warn't dead. I was ever so glad to see Jim. I warn't lonesome now. I told him I warn't afraid of HIM telling the people where I was."

Maybe Stone was lonesome too and needed a "fren." Yet the only folks he trusted were priests. Unlikely that he would trust Gabriel—and for good reason: Even Gabriel himself was unsure how he would handle Stone if he found him. It depended largely on Stone and how reasonable—or unreasonable—he was. But of course Gabriel didn't yet know where he was.

That thought made him back up a few pages to find out exactly where Huck was. He had gone to the far shore of Jackson's Island, facing the Illinois side of the river.

Gabriel found an online aerial map that confirmed what he had observed, damn little on the Illinois shore except for largely unpeopled bottomland. A few small towns south, Quincy, larger, a few miles north.

If Stone, the born-again Catholic who ordered fish on Friday, had not gone to Mass at Holy Family in Hannibal on Sunday or taken confession previously with the Dallas Cowboy cheerleader Father Salas, he likely did it somewhere else. So he typed in a search for nearby Catholic churches.

Just north of Hannibal in Palmyra, Missouri, he found St. Joseph's Catholic Church. And, closer still, just across the Mississippi at Quincy's southern edge, St. Anthony of Padua Catholic Church.

Gabriel smiled and leaned back in his chair. "Bingo!" he said aloud. "'Something's lost and can't be found / Please, St. Anthony, look around.' Thank you, Father Mohan!"

Stone, fond of masks, subterfuge, and wordplay—and seemingly trying to find himself—might be lured by such serendipity.

Gabriel clicked through to the website and learned the church conducted weekday Masses Monday, Tuesday, and Thursday mornings at seven-thirty. He left a wakeup call for six.

Then he opened the bottle of whiskey he carried in his briefcase, found an NBA game on the TV, and called out for pizza. Fuck the diet. He felt good about this hunch—cause to celebrate. He sipped iced bourbon from a plastic cup, put his feet up on the bed, muted the TV, and cracked open *English Grammar for Idiots*.

§

Gabriel drew back the hotel room drapes. Morning again came gray and cold. He checked his email and looked at the weather online. It was as The Gecko had said, more snow coming in from the Plains.

Gabriel paid his bill at the front desk, found his Dodge in the parking lot, and headed north out of Hannibal. He took the new bridge—new to him at least—and crossed the Mississippi into Illinois. There he traversed flat, denuded bottomland, brown and unwelcoming. He followed the highway as it bent north, and soon left the interstate for the old highway and found Saint Anthony Road.

The church was modern, located just southeast of Quincy—more of a metropolis than Hannibal, with some forty thousand inhabitants. A dozen cars rested in the parking lot outside the church. As he walked to the sanctuary a westerly wind cut through his overcoat.

Inside, the parishioners were mostly gray-haired women, a few elderly men. No Stone, though he was early. Gabriel genuflected, crossed himself, and sat in a back pew. Another half dozen elderly joined the worshippers, and after a few more minutes Gabriel looked at his watch, seven thirty-five. When he looked up, Stone was moving down the aisle toward a seat in the middle of the sanctuary.

He wore dark slacks and a brown corduroy sport coat with professorial elbow-patches. He sported a burgeoning blonde beard that made him look like an Anglicized Christ.

Gabriel launched a brief silent prayer: "Thank you, Saint Anthony, for your help and guidance."

The priest, a tall, burly, and balding middle-aged man, entered to organ music and went to the altar. Soon he turned to the congregation.

"In the name of the Father, and of the Son, and of the Holy Spirit."

"Amen," came the response as all made the sign of the cross.

"The grace and peace of God our Father and the Lord Jesus Christ be with you."

"And also with you."

The priest introduced the holy water and sprinkled it about the worshippers.

How long had it been since Gabriel had sat through a Mass? Other than weddings, a long time. The Mass proceeded: the kyrie, the gloria, the prayers, the liturgy, all of which he tuned out, focusing on Stone.

Longish blond hair curling down to his jacket collar, rimless eyeglasses, gaunt, with chiseled features. Gabriel saw how a Hannibal waitress might find him exotic. When the communion rite began at the altar, Stone participated. Gabriel stayed put. It had been but scant days since his confession to Father Mohan, but he doubted he was still in a state of grace.

"The peace of the Lord be with you always."

"And with your spirit."

"Have mercy on us. Grant us peace. Grant us peace."

"Behold the Lamb of God … supper of the Lamb."

"Lord, I am not worthy that you should enter under my roof, but only say the word and my soul shall be healed…."

As Stone returned to his seat, their eyes met for an instant. He didn't look haunted, like a man on the run. He looked peaceful. Or maybe quietly insane.

After the service Gabriel watched Stone grab his parka from the coat rack in the vestibule and move outside looking over his shoulder. The professor stiff-legged it across the plowed parking lot toward a gray, twenty-year-old Chevrolet with a temporary tag taped in the back window. Gabriel loped after him in his slick-soled Italian loafers, side-stepping patches of ice. Stone flung open the door, lurched behind the steering wheel, and ground the starter. As Gabriel approached, the engine fired, a cloud of blue smoke bursting from its tailpipe.

Stone threw the Chevy in gear. Gabriel raised his badge in front of the windshield.

"Police! Turn off the fucking engine."

Their eyes met again through the glass. After a couple beats Stone lowered his head, shoulders sagging, and reached to kill the motor. Gabriel felt someone staring at him and turned to see a half dozen aged parishioners huddled together across the parking lot, mouths agape. He turned back and yanked open the car door.

"Jonathan Stone ... I've been searching for you."

Stone looked him up and down. "Friend or foe?"

Gabriel shrugged. "Let's pray for the former."

§

In a booth at a downtown Quincy diner, Stone looked out the window to a park with tall oaks. Snow had begun to fall, and the bare branches wore a light sprinkling of white.

"It was here, detective, in Washington Park, that Lincoln debated Douglas. Mark Twain—Sam Clemens then—would have been twenty-two, apprenticing as a riverboat pilot. Those debates are not unrelated to my work on Twain. Lincoln said, 'I believe this government cannot endure permanently half slave and half free.' *Adventures of Huckleberry Finn*—set twenty years before abolition and published twenty years after—rephrased Lincoln's posit. And now a hundred years after Twain's death it still needs saying."

"So I gathered from your writing."

"What writing?"

"'Corruption in the public schools,' 'Corruption in academia.'"

"You found those?"

A waitress arrived with water, coffee, and menus. When she had poured and left, Gabriel said:

"Not me. Another officer."

Stone stroked his beard. "I guess I was naïve. Always had my nose buried in books. That's what interested me and seemed of utmost importance. But then I got these students—ambitious inner-city kids who were trying to do something for themselves. They had been stoked with all these dreams but given none of the tools to achieve them. And when they spoke … when they spoke you could hear echoes of the runaway slave Jim."

Gabriel blew on his coffee and sipped. "You ran away too."

"I was facing some issues. Still am. As you likely know, I lost my job. Then there were some personal issues. It seemed time for me to spend forty days and forty nights in the wilderness."

"Issues like your wife's unfaithfulness and criminal activity, which I was going over again last night."

"You found that too?"

"The Gecko's good. He's our resident geek."

"I guess it doesn't matter now that I've made up my mind. At first I wasn't sure what to do with all that. Despite her unfaithfulness, Ellen is still my wife. But not exposing what's going on downtown—given that I could figure some effective way to do it—would be a sin of omission I wouldn't want to live with."

Gabriel heaved a deep sigh and shook his head.

"That's a problem for you, detective?"

The waitress returned and took their orders. When she had gone, Gabriel picked up his spoon and stirred his coffee. After a moment, he said, "I suspect that would make the mayor very unhappy."

"No shit, Sherlock."

"And it would put you on Front Street."

"I understand that."

"I don't think you do. You don't understand how they operate downtown. They play hard. Angelo Cira is not Mafia but his uncle was. And he's a tough ex-cop and -prosecutor."

"Meaning what? He would send some goon to 'rub me out' or whatever the phrase? Hard to believe."

"There's a lot at stake here, Stone. Have you been to your cloud accounts in the last few days?"

"No. Why?"

"They—whoever 'they' are—have gone in and emptied them and are covering the electronic tracks you found. Plus

I'm sure they're putting tremendous pressure on your wife, for whatever that's worth to you."

Gabriel decided his coffee needed sugar and poured some from a jar on the table before continuing. "Perhaps it's better just to drop it. Go home, try to patch things up with the wife, focus on literature and language. That's what you know best."

Stone leaned forward, forearms on the table cordoning his coffee cup. "But don't you see they're all related. They're stealing money from the charter schools and mismanaging the rest, and it's the students who pay the price. Your boss Cira is set to make millions on the backs of kids who don't have a square chance. And it seems that you're playing along too."

"I'm a realist, you're an idealist. Everybody fudges. Ninety-eight percent of us manipulate our tax returns and insurance claims. We roll through stop signs and go five miles over the speed limit. We give customers more than they wanted and charge them for it. We all cheat just a little to give us an edge or help the team, but not enough to feel bad about ourselves. Maybe there's one percent that never cheats and another percent that cheats big time—those are the ones my kind generally go after. It's the way of the world, human nature. It's how things work."

"But in this case, it's not working. Kids are getting screwed. Everyone has only one chance in life to be young, to get the education needed to have even half a chance to succeed. These people are taking that one chance away and leaving these kids nothing. We have laws and covenants designed to help us rise above our nature. But they have to be enforced and followed and engrained in our culture, or ultimately we all lose. That's not idealistic, that's pragmatic."

The waitress returned with ham, eggs, hash browns, toast, and more coffee. Gabriel thought it a good time to redirect the conversation and save what he really needed to say for later, when they were alone and he could make his case more emphatically.

"You were not an easy man to find, professor. No electronic trail whatsoever. Must have planned your escape."

Stone shook his head as he chewed. "Not at all. But it was as if Providence had a hand in it. I'd lost my job on Friday. That night I watched Ellen and her lover Cira together at the Christmas party. You can imagine what was going through my mind. Maybe you don't have to imagine if you've read 'The Eddy.' Some very primal and ugly currents swirling around inside me. I tried to get on top of those feelings and not let them degrade me and pull me down. I wasn't successful."

Gabriel poked at his food and listened, watching Stone's face.

"When we got home, she went to the kitchen to swallow down some aspirins. I told her we had to talk. She said not tonight, she was tired. But I persisted. Told her I wanted to renew our marriage, to re-devote ourselves to each other. I remember her exact words:

"'You're joking.'"

"I told her I could forgive her for whatever she'd done, but that we had to start over fresh. Her reaction was to berate me. 'What? *You* forgive *me?*' She asked what had I ever contributed to the marriage. Told me to grow up, climb down out of my ivory tower, to stop living in a fantasy world. Then she turned and walked to the bedroom.

"I didn't sleep much. I lay there staring at her back, thinking of Cira's hands on her. She had changed. Over the years, the access to power had altered her. The more people kissed her ass, the more she expected it from me. It was all about her. An intolerable situation for me.

"I rose early and chronicled the events of the previous day in my journal. Then I took a look at the newspaper and read that a student of mine had been shot."

"Alonzo Watkins."

"How do you know about him?"

"I met with Letty Tatum. She told me."

Stone raised his eyebrows. "My, you have been on the job. No Stone left unreturned."

"You were saying,..."

"After I read about Alonzo I called the hospital but didn't learn much. I exchanged emails with a priest who had been counseling me—"

"Father Mohan."

"Right. And made an appointment for him to hear my confession that afternoon. I took a walk through Forest Park in the snow. It was beautiful. Hundreds of snow geese were on the ice near the boathouse, huddled together, quiet. Anyway, I trudged over to Barnes to see Alonzo, but he was in intensive care. I found out he'd been shot in the back, lung collapsed, but out of danger. I left a note for him, then drove to Saint Louis U., had a late lunch at a nearby pub, and met with Father Mohan. He heard my confession and gave me some good advice that reminded me of my duty to serve."

"I got the same lecture."

"It was dark when I came out. I drove around. I had so

much churning around inside me ... I ended up downtown. Went to the rooftop bar at the Marriott across from the ballpark. I looked down on where Stadium Towne would go, thinking about what Cira was skimming from the project and Ellen's complicity in it, and the dropouts roaming the streets without jobs or prospects. I had a few Irish whiskeys—okay, more than a few—and needed some fresh air." He paused and Gabriel waited, still watching Stone's face, trying to get a sense of how set the man was on going public. Stone continued.

"I walked across the street to the Old Courthouse. Stood there studying the statue of Dred Scott and his wife. That's where they first petitioned for their freedom."

Gabriel nodded. "Learned about that in school."

"Without them Lincoln may have never become president, the Civil War may not have been fought—at least then—and Twain may not have written *Huck Finn*. Who knows what effect any action has downstream, I thought, even the smallest ripple. I wasn't ready to go home, so I crossed to the Arch and walked through it and down the steps to the river. All of it was stirring inside—Mark Twain and the river, Huck and Jim, Ellen and Cira, DuWayne Hawkins and Betancourt, Alonzo, the corruption and the kickbacks, the schools being robbed, the kids getting fucked out of any real chance in life. The whole world seemed tainted—me included. My career a shambles, my marriage a wreck. Worse, my wife was up to her chin in a criminal conspiracy, and I didn't know where my duty lay—or my loyalties. Didn't know if I had the guts to expose her or if I should, or whether I would just join in the corruption. I was humiliated. I was a nobody, a loser, ineffectual....

"I stood on the cobblestones at the river's edge, drunk and crying. I'd lost my way. My life seemed so pointless and useless. Then I saw him. I must have sensed movement out the corner of my eye."

"You saw the jumper?"

Stone looked up at Gabriel and held his gaze. "He was standing on the railing of Eads Bridge. Poised there with arms stretched like Christ on the cross. Spontaneously I yelled, 'Don't!'—though I'm sure he couldn't hear me. He began tilting forward as if in slow motion, then the free fall. He hit the water hard. I guess seeing someone die is nothing to you."

"That's not an easy thing to witness for anyone."

"It was horrific. Suicide is a mortal sin."

"I know, I'm Catholic, too."

"A car was parked on the wharf, windows steamed. A young black guy jumped out zipping his pants. He looked at me. 'Damn! You see that?' We stood on the bank scouring the river, but what with the ice floes and the dark…"

Stone shook his head and took in a breath.

"His girlfriend came out the other side of the car. I asked if they had a cell phone. She called 911. I felt sick. I sat down on the curb, leaning against a post. I saw the guy telling his girlfriend something. They got back in the car and drove off. I waited.

"After awhile a police car came. I figured they would want to talk to me. But the car just drove past slowly and didn't even stop. Maybe they didn't see me sitting there.

"I sat staring at the river as if hoping the jumper might resurface, resurrected. I sat thinking what a gift life is, and how ephemeral. And how I was wasting mine. A bad marriage, stupid career choices, a naïve intellectuality that got me nowhere. A cuckold. A nothing."

"Yeah, you had a couple rough days."

Stone looked askance at Gabriel. "I suspect your job makes you blasé and cynical."

"Sorry. I wasn't being sarcastic. I didn't mean to diminish your problems and your suffering. But maybe you're being too hard on yourself. You weren't the one cheating. Your head was being messed with, but your heart was in the right place."

"For all the good that does. You know how a man's judged in this world, detective, not by what's in his heart but by what he does. Twain said it: "The streets of Hell are paved with good intentions." For once, I needed to act. But it had to be the right action. And I needed time to figure out what it ought to be."

"And you thought of Huck."

"I wasn't thinking clearly but, yeah, that somehow came to me as I sat wondering about the man in the river and what might have driven him to it. I recalled how Huck had orchestrated the appearance of his demise—his own disappearance in the river—to escape his father. If Ellen thought she'd lost me—if she felt the same thing I had felt seeing that man die, if she realized what a sacred treasure we have in life—maybe she'd come to her senses and do the right thing. At the same time, I'm sure I wanted to hurt her and saw the potential to damage Angelo Cira as well. But I didn't know if I should—or could.

"Thus my decision to go walkabout. I sat there in the snow figuring how to do it, how to disappear like Huck. If I left Ellen's car in the Arch garage, that might associate me with the jumper as long as there was no further trace of me. Which of course ruled out credit cards, plane tickets, Internet presence, cell phones, et cetera.

"I took the MetroLink home. I knew Ellen would be off at some political function. I had some cash hidden away—money I'd been secretly saving for years from freelance work, book reviews, and such. Almost four thousand."

"For just such an occasion?"

Stone laughed coldly. "We never had a honeymoon. Got married when we were grad students. Then she started working at the TV station, and we never seemed to have time. When she went to work for the mayor I thought we could finally do it. I wanted to surprise her. But she surprised me first.

"Anyway, I got the money and went on her computer. Mark Twain as always was on my brain, along with my dissertation. I figured to finally finish it with some uninterrupted work over the next few weeks and thought Hannibal might help me evoke him. I found that a Trailways bus would leave the airport for Hannibal at seven-fifty Sunday morning. I left my cell phone behind and took the train to the airport. I spent the night in the terminal dozing in a chair alongside other passengers.

"Next morning the bus ride in the snow calmed me and fortified me. Rural America is still beautiful, still solid. I knocked around Hannibal for a few days and bought the Chevy off a used car lot for twelve hundred bucks. Saw an ad in the newspaper for weekly rates at a hotel in Quincy and passed St. Anthony's on the way, where I started going to Mass."

"Patron saint of missing persons."

"Of course that occurred to me. A little too clever perhaps."

"Just as well. I needed to find you."

"I can guess why. Cira sent you."

Gabriel shrugged. "Your wife's also worried about you. At least now I can reassure her that you're all right. But there's more to it than that."

"What is your role here, detective?"

The waitress brought the check and Gabriel reached for it. "I'd like to play St. Christopher and carry you safely to the other shore. But that may not be that simple."

- 22 -

The snow whipped around them as they walked through the park where Lincoln debated Douglas. They turned and headed down toward the river. No traffic, an eerie quiet.

"Thanks for breakfast," said Stone from beneath the hood of his olive parka.

"Expense account. Besides, you're on a budget."

"For the time being."

"Prospects?"

"Got a job starting in a few weeks teaching English at a charter high school in North St. Louis. A colleague there hooked me up."

"Sounds right for you."

"Even though I haven't yet started, it feels like a calling."

On the riverfront the snow streamed in from the Missouri side. There they found a tavern that was just opening for lunch.

Once inside, Gabriel stomped snow from his shoes and brushed it from his hair. They ordered whiskey shots— Jack Daniel's for Gabriel, Jameson for Stone—and sat on barstools staring at The Weather Channel on a muted TV over the bar. The satellite map showed white, snow, over northern Missouri and Illinois and blue, ice, further south.

Gabriel lifted his shot toward the screen. "Looks messy."

"So much for St. Christopher. Seems we're both stuck here."

Gabriel studied him. "I'm not so sure. Maybe there's a way out for you, Stone."

"Meaning a way out for you."

"Hear me out. We can both come out of this on top. When you first disappeared I did some digging into what may have motivated you. I learned what your students thought of you and what you were doing to help them get on. I saw how you stood your ground with that jackass Betancourt. And I read your research into the public school fiasco— compelling stuff. This is all to the good, even your getting sacked. Puts you in a position where you can perhaps serve best. But none of that will mean a thing if you're prevented from doing your work—one way or another.

"I don't like the sound of that."

"Even though the charter schools have some autonomy, they're still run by the city, and Angelo Cira still runs the city. Any number of ways he could screw with you and endanger your gig there and maybe even endanger you. If you persist in outing the mayor and your wife on Stadium Towne, you're putting yourself in an extremely precarious position. You might get a warning and you might not."

"I thought that's what this was."

Gabriel looked again at the satellite map. "Let me give you the big picture." He turned back to Stone. "Do you still have that digital recorder you used on Betancourt?"

"Back in my hotel room."

"Open your coat."

Stone smiled and spread the lapels of his corduroy jacket.

Gabriel glanced at the bartender's back, reached across, and patted Stone down but found only a cell phone and a wallet.

"Okay. Confession time," said Gabriel. "Pretend you're a priest and keep this under your hat. Angelo Cira and I worked together some thirty years ago. I was with him when he shot and killed a black perp in a takedown. Except the guy was unarmed."

"You saw Cira kill an unarmed man? Then why isn't he in prison?"

Gabriel set his glass down a little too sharply and the bartender turned to see if there was trouble. Gabriel smiled and waved him away. "Just shut up for a minute, professor. Listen and learn. Maybe Ange thought he was going for a gun and panicked—we were young cops. That's the charitable view."

"And the uncharitable?"

"There was some history between the dead man and Cira. He'd busted him earlier and words were exchanged. Ange thumped him, as was customary then—these were the days before goddamn digital cameras—and got spit on for his efforts. To some who knew that history it looked like payback time, and some didn't care.

"But I was the only one who saw it go down. Cira planted a gun on him. 'We're not black and white, Carlo,' he said. 'We're cops. We stick together. That's the code.' So I played along. I went to confession about it, but that didn't help. I told Cira. He says, 'The guy was a punk. You'll get over it.' Apparently *he* already had."

Stone sipped his whiskey. "And the seeming purpose of this parable—perhaps apocryphal—is to intimidate me."

"Let's say 'educate' you."

"'Don't rat out the mayor and your life will be spared.' Is that your offer? You'll have to do better than that."

Gabriel shook a finger at him. "I knew masochistic mofos like you at Catholic school, all wrapped up in some martyr complex. You want to hang on a cross half naked and have virgins swoon at your feet."

"Either you got it or you don't."

"Surprised you aren't a priest."

"Only one deadly sin stood between me and the priesthood—lust. That and my pheromones."

"What the hell's that?"

"Sexual chemistry, detective. Some guys attract women with big bank accounts or appendages. I have big pheromones."

Gabriel laughed. "So that's why the waitress at the diner across the river had the hots for you."

This time, Stone laughed. "Strange isn't it, but it happens all the time."

"I wish you weren't such a stubborn son of a bitch. I think we'd get along."

"I don't think you wish that, not in your heart."

"I think I know what's in your heart. You want to work with those kids. And as a good Catholic you want to save your marriage. Sending your wife to prison won't help you achieve either goal. But you hold a hell of bargaining chip with her. I suspect she's gotten in way over her head and may be looking for a way out. You can offer a helping hand."

Stone thought for a moment and said: "I would think a savvy prosecutor might have more to offer her, including a way to stay out of prison and serve society by serving up Angelo Cira."

"You're dreaming, Stone." He lifted his chin toward the TV. "Watching too much *Law & Order*. I can't see City Hall letting things get that far."

"Thanks for the threat, but for some reason you don't scare me. You don't seem the violent sort."

"Wait till I get more whiskey in me."

"By the way, what's in it for you?"

"Let's say my fortunes are tied to those of the mayor."

"That'll be unfortunate when he goes under."

"You mean 'if' and that's a big if. But I'm a survivor. Just hope we all can survive this."

Gabriel's cell phone dinged: a text message from The Gecko: "Call me. Urgent." He looked to Stone.

"The cell phone in your coat pocket—is it linked to you?"

"No. Prepaid. And I've disabled the GPS."

"Let's have it."

He dialed The Gecko's safe number. Before he could say a word, he heard, "Carlo, Ellen Cantrell is dead."

Garbriel stiffened. His eyes moved to Stone, then to the unvarnished wood slat floor. He took in a breath.

"How?"

The Gecko told him what he knew, it wasn't much. Gabriel signed off, handed the phone back to Stone, and waved a twenty at the bartender.

Outside on the sidewalk the blowing snow encircled them. Stone was pulling on his gloves. "What's the sudden hurry?"

Gabriel looked out across a barren park toward the gray river swirling by not fifty yards distant, relentless as death itself. He reached out and laid a glove on the arm of Stone's parka.

"I've got some bad news for you, Jonathan. It's your wife."

"Ellen? What?"

"She's … She's dead."

Stone stood staring at Gabriel, jaw slack, the snow now clinging to his eyeglasses, clouding his gaze.

"Dead?" He shook his head in disbelief. "Who says?"

Gabriel sensed the murmur of the river sluicing by. "Second District patrol found her in Forest Park, in her car. A gunshot wound to the head, self-inflicted. I'm sorry, Jonathan."

Stone brought his hands to his ears, as if trying to silence Gabriel, and dropped to his knees in the blowing snow. He leaned back, seemingly to howl, but no noise emitted from his throat.

As usual, Gabriel had no idea what to do or say. Everything he could say—my condolences, be brave, she's gone to a better place, buck up, or whatever—seemed clichéd (he'd read about clichés in his grammar book the night before) and insipid. So he turned away, another mute.

Then a sob broke from Stone. Gabriel turned back to see him scrambling to his feet then bolting across the street toward the park, sliding over the railroad crossing at the corner and heading for the rushing river. Gabriel tore after him.

But Gabriel's Ferragamos gave poor traction in the snow—he slipped and stumbled to one knee, painfully, in the street. He rose, kicked off his loafers, and raced after Stone in stocking feet.

But Stone was staggering, not sprinting toward the river. He moved as if inebriated—drunk on sorrow, drunk on guilt. Gabriel caught him at the river's edge before he could take the plunge—if that's what he was intending—embracing him in a bear hug and pulling him away from the water.

"Easy, Stone, easy."

Gabriel held him, feeling him clinging and shaking in his arms like a child.

- 23 -

Days earlier Jonathan Stone had taken a musty room in an old downtown Quincy hotel that rented "Efficiency apartments by the week and month," according to a sign out front. Now he lay on the green vinyl loveseat—head on one worn armrest, calves on the other. Gabriel sat at an old wooden desk searching the St. Louis Metropolitan Police Department I/LEADS website from his laptop. Over his shoulder he stole a look at Stone, who seemed better now that the initial shock and grief had come and gone. Gabriel, too, felt better since he had muddled through his usual inept performance as bearer of bad news. He turned back to his computer. After a minute he said, "Here it is."

"Read it to me."

"I'm not sure you want to hear all the details."

"Read it."

"The idiots can't write—misplaced modifiers, comma splices … I'll paraphrase. White female discovered in a late-model Ford SUV, property of the City of St. Louis, at 5:45 this morning in Forest Park near the Muny Opera parking lot. Engine running, doors unlocked. One fatal shot to the right temple apparently fired at close range from a Seecamp 32 found at the scene and registered to the victim. No signs of struggle. Purse containing credit cards and some two hundred dollars in cash on the passenger seat. 'Nothing to suggest that the wound was other than self-inflicted'—quote, unquote."

Stone pulled himself up and went to the window. "I pulled the trigger."

"Don't, Jonathan."

"Morally I'm responsible. I abandoned her. I wanted her to suffer. My actions precipitated this."

Gabriel turned to him. "It seems to me she abandoned you. Put herself in the situation that led to this."

"How goddamn selfish to run off without a word. What was I thinking?"

"Let me see what I can find out before you start nailing yourself up. This may be related to something else."

A gooseneck lamp lit the desk where Gabriel sat. Feeble gray afternoon light came from the window where Stone stood.

"Is that what you think? That it's nothing to do with me? Just coincidence?"

"I'm not saying it doesn't have anything to do with you, but we need to know what's really going on before we draw any conclusions. Before we know what to do. Your phone?"

He lifted his chin toward the Formica-topped coffee table by the loveseat, where his cell phone lay amid newspapers and books. Gabriel grabbed it and dialed. After a few buzzes he got a voice mail message and said:

"Laura, Carlo. Give me a call back at this number ASAP. Urgent, relating to Ellen Cantrell."

Gabriel went back to his laptop. Laura Berkman called within minutes.

"I'm working on a story now," she said, "waiting for relatives to be notified before identifying her by name."

"Off the record, I can help with that."

"You found him? Where are you?"

"Can't say. When I can, you come first. In the meantime, whatever you can turn up on this could be helpful. Including who's handling the investigation. As well as any rumors. Any detail could be crucial."

"I don't like the sound of that."

"Yeah, well I don't like saying it, either. And don't tell anyone we talked. Seriously. No one." His own cell phone began beeping on the desk. "I gotta go."

He returned to the desk and studied the caller I.D.: Captain Elijah Hancock, Seventh District commander, who was Gabriel's nominal supervisor while detached from headquarters and, at this moment, a likely pipeline from the mayor. He decided he better answer.

"Gabriel, you hear the news?"

"Yeah."

"You making any headway finding the husband?"

He looked at Stone. "He's alive. I've been communicating with him and informed him of his wife's death. Now I'm trying to coax him in."

"Good work. I'll let the mayor know."

"Tell him I have everything under control."

When he hung up, Stone swung his legs off the couch and looked at him and said, "Now what?"

"I don't know."

"I need a drink."

Gabriel went to his briefcase on the floor beside the desk and withdrew the fifth of bourbon. Stone got glasses.

Gabriel turned the desk chair around, sat, and raised his glass.

"My condolences, Jonathan."

"I'm trying to picture her. Where is she now?"

"Likely the city morgue."

"I meant spiritually. Suicide's a grave sin. I pray there's a merciful God."

"As do we all."

Stone sat on the loveseat and drank. He looked to the ceiling, tears welling.

"She really wowed me when we met. Eager, ambitious, bold. A good complement to my introversion. She looked up to me. We helped each other, pushed each other, strove together. And drifted apart."

"Sounds like she did most of the drifting ... What did her parents say when you called?"

Stone lifted his eyeglasses and wiped away tears with the back of his hand. "I talked with her father. What could he say? He never much cared for me. Thought she could have done better—i.e., a Protestant lawyer or doctor. He'll feel vindicated in that opinion once I blow the whistle on her."

Gabriel set his glass on the coffee table. "What the hell you talking about?"

"There's nothing stopping me now. Her death will be rendered meaningless if I don't act."

"Slow down. Give it some time. You're emotional and not making good decisions. Besides, all the research and documentation you had in the cloud has evaporated. You've got nothing to go with."

"Detective...."

"Professor."

"What do you want me to call you?"

"Lieutenant Gabriel, to be correct. But I'd prefer Carlo or just Gabriel."

"Carlo, do you know how we succeed in life? By acquiring property and wealth? By earning trophies? By gratifying our sensual selves? No, by helping people. By serving."

"I know you're in a sentimental mood, Stone, but you're starting to sound like my old man."

"Ask any business owner, any teacher, any honest cop."

"So you say."

"Nietzsche was right, evil springs from weakness. The world's wickedness is not perpetrated by malevolent devils but by the cumulative effects of our own moral failings and cowardice. Giving an undeserving student a passing grade, bending rules to please superiors, cheating on your spouse, taking a kickback, doctoring your product, cutting corners, hiring your friend or mistress instead of someone more qualified—"

"Human nature. We're born sinners."

"But we don't have to die that way. I can't fix all the corruption in the world, but I can fix what's inside me—or at least try. Maybe then I can help fix what's broken in our schools. And maybe then we can throw the moneychangers out of government. Who knows? But I suggest we start now."

Gabriel picked up the bottle and poured himself more whiskey. "What do you mean 'we,' white man?"

"I mean I need your help and complicity."

Gabriel held up a hand. "Hold it right there. I'm not looking to change the world. I just want to get my rank back and cruise on toward Pensionville. Five years and out."

"Then what?"

"You don't want to know."

"Tell me."

"I too plan to go into education, schooling lovely brown-eyed, honey-skinned Mexican ladies half my age."

"Not exactly what I meant by service."

Stone reached for the bottle, poured himself another, and leaned across to top off Gabriel's drink. His cell phone buzzed, and Gabriel grabbed it, looked at the number, and pressed a button.

"Hey Laura, what did you find out?"

"Embargo's lifted and the story's hitting electronic media now. The mayor's closeted. Chief Donnewald's acting spokesman and issued a statement. 'The mayor and everyone at City Hall are devastated by this personal tragedy,'" she read. "'We ask that the news media respect the privacy of her family members and friends during this difficult period.' In other words, nothing political here, just a troubled young woman with too much stress taking her own life—and don't bother talking to her husband. Let's move on."

"Who's handling the investigation?"

"Donnewald himself, 'given the sensitive nature of this tragedy.'"

"In other words, more snow on the way."

He hung up and recounted the conversation to Stone. He reached for the TV remote. "Want to see what they're saying on TV?"

Stone shook his head. "I'd rather hear what you have to say."

Gabriel pursed his lips and set the remote back on the table.

Stone stood up and started pacing. "When did you say my files were wiped from the cloud?"

"Three or four days ago."

"Yet at breakfast this morning you said you were going back over some of the material last night."

"I said that?"

"Yes, you did."

Now Gabriel poured them both more whiskey. "Okay, honest cop here. I've got a couple flash drives with everything on them. But I planned on chucking those into the Mississippi on the way back."

Stone stopped and looked down at him. "I've a better idea. Let's email the contents to your friend Laura Berkman. I know she covers City Hall for the paper. And we can post it all on the Web."

Gabriel drank down a dollop of liquor. "You may think you have nothing to lose since you don't seem to value your own life, but I do."

"There's more at stake here than our personal fortunes."

"Speak for yourself."

Stone studied Gabriel. "Okay, I will... Last semester, maybe the third week of class, my grammar students were haunting me. I was doing what I could, but they just weren't getting it. I was beginning to think maybe they couldn't get it. Maybe that was the reason the public schools had passed them on. They really were just dim. Or after years of suffering from educational malpractice they had grown slow, their faculties atrophied.

"Then one day when it was hot as hell I went into the student union to get an iced tea. And there was one of my grammar students sitting by himself at a table with a small chessboard in front of him, working through some endgame puzzle from the newspaper—Alonzo Watkins.

"He asked if I wanted to play. I told him it had been a while but I'd try. I was number one board on my high-school team and figured to teach him a thing or two. When he reached into his backpack, brought out a chess clock, and said, 'Five minutes each,' I sensed trouble.

"I started with a Queen's Gambit, which he quickly tore up. And Alonzo didn't just move his pieces, he slam-dunked them. My flag fell, which saved me getting mated. I told him I was little rusty and suggested another match. He shrugged as if indifferent.

"This time, as if to further humiliate me as he kicked my ass, he added play-by-play. 'Teacher man go queen to h5, into the deep shit. Zo go BAM! and take the black bitch.'"

Gabriel smiled. His dad had been ruthless at chess, always playing with a take-no-prisoners attitude.

"Afterward I asked where he learned to play," Stone continued. "You know what he told me?"

"What?"

"Barbershops in North St. Louis. Who would have thought? But why not? Why was that so surprising to me?"

"'Cause you're a white man," Gabriel said. "Not that there's anything wrong with that, but…."

Stone didn't seem to get the humor and just kept on going. "Exactly. So I learned two lessons. First, I realized I had come to expect failure from Alonzo and students like him just because he was black and from North St. Louis. Second, I saw he was not a young man with diminished intellect. I saw that the problem wasn't with him but with me and his other teachers. Still, I had no idea how to teach him and the others what they needed to know.

"But soon, with some student intervention, we found a solution. We decided to go back to where the problem started—first grade—and launching from there. We all learned in that class. I hadn't realized how really complex English grammar could be, the stuff we do more or less automatically every day.

"But here's the biggest lesson for us, Carlo: There are a million more Alonzos out there who have to be taught what every English-speaking kid in the world needs to know: the conventions of the language. They need to be able to communicate effectively in the public sphere and actuate themselves, to free themselves from the last lingering shackles of slavery. To deny them that opportunity is criminal."

"You're seeing crime everywhere, Stone. But how about this? Some folks might say it's criminal to rob them of their black dialect. That all you're talking about is white patriarchy."

Stone waved it away. "They can talk however they want at home and on the street. I know third generation Americans who still speak Italian at home, but they know how to read, speak, and write Standard English."

"Yeah, but by whose standards?"

"The consensus. The language of our textbooks, instruction manuals, legislation, and news reports. None of it's written in black dialect or creole or Spanglish. As expressive as they might be, they're not much use in acing job interviews, writing business contracts, or giving control-tower instructions. By whatever historical accident, effort, and ruthlessness, English rules. People from all over the

world—and I've had students from all corners—understand
that and learn the formal language. And when they do, they
move to the head of the class, stepping right over our inner-
city kids on the way."

"Yeah, yeah. I hear you. But no one stepped over me.
I came from 'the ghetto,' and there were a lot of decent
families like mine, a lot of good people. Lots of my friends
went to public school and fared all right."

"But that was forty, fifty years ago. The cultural
circumstances have changed."

"You going to lecture me about that as well? Now you
think you know everything about the 'hood? Just like the
rest of the do-gooders and university types, you want to sit
above it all and tell us what's best for us."

Gabriel got up to take a piss. The bathroom window
had been left half open and snow had accumulated on the
sill. He could see the towering superstructure of the bridge
spanning the Mississippi, which flowed gray and urgent
beneath it. The view, as much as the cold air, chilled him,
and he pushed the window closed.

When he returned, Stone started in again. "Look, Carlo.
I know there are still good families. People trying to do
right by their kids and students hungry for an education.
But through no fault of their own they aren't getting it.
Many know they're getting shafted but don't understand
why. And maybe what I'm getting is all secondary research
and hearsay, but a lot of it comes from the mouths and the
hearts of my students. They're the ones who've taught me.
Which is why I'm leaving the ivory tower and getting down
in the trenches. I can't turn my back on these kids. And I
don't think you can either."

"Watch me. I'm no teacher, just a cop. My job is to find you—which I've done—and to see you don't make waves. Which I think I can achieve by consigning your files to the Father of Waters."

"Don't you feel anything for your people?"

"Ah, the race card. Hardly a trump in my case. The world will go on its merry, corrupt way no matter what I do. I'm looking out for number one."

"So are the people you arrest."

"Up yours, professor."

Stone took a drink. "You ever read *Invisible Man*?"

"Saw the movie."

"Not *The Invisible Man*. Ralph Ellison's book. His advice was to go easy and keep on helping your people—but don't go too fast or they will cut you down."

"You don't know shit about being black. Or Mexican. Or poor."

"But Ralph Ellison did. And I can read what he had to say about it and share his experience. I can grow by it and profit by it. But those kids who are falling through the cracks can't even do that. They can't read it *because they can't read*. Many of them are functionally illiterate and some can't read beyond a fourth or fifth grade level. You can help fix that, Carlo, by helping me to expose the corruption and shine a light on these problems. Here's a chance to do something principled and serve your people. Help me with this. Make a difference. Maybe you won't get your rank back—"

"No 'maybe' about it."

"But you'll get something more important."

"Do tell, professor. What will I get?"

"I think you know."

"Spell it out."

"Your self-respect."

Gabriel felt himself color, ears burning. He rose and poured more whiskey into his glass.

"You don't know shit about me, Stone. And you don't know what you're getting into."

"Educate me."

Gabriel drank. "I already told you that we need to know what's really going on before we draw any conclusions. Before we know what to do. But here you are drawing conclusions and deciding what to do before we know anything at all."

"We know we have a chance to help these kids, and that's the only thing that's important right now."

"The only thing, huh? There's one other thing you're not taking into account. Something you should give careful consideration to, but from your martyred, self-righteous perch, you can't even see."

"What's that?"

"Maybe it's just the suspicious cop in me, but I don't think your wife killed herself."

Stone stared at him. "Explain."

Now it was Gabriel's turn to pace. "First, her car was found in an out-of-the-way spot in Forest Park. A venue that's off the beaten path, without a lot of through-traffic. A place where highly recognizable public figures might be able to have a private conversation without being spotted. And a dark place to commit murder without witnesses.

"Second, the doors were unlocked. Nowadays doors lock automatically when you drive. Which suggests the possibility that someone got into or out of the car after it was parked. Nonetheless, we get the case file editorializing that there's no reason to suspect that the wound was anything other than self-inflicted. Also no mention of any footprints in the snow around the vehicle or lack of such, so bad detective work right there.

"Third, who's personally overseeing the investigation? Police Chief Donnewald himself. Highly irregular. And we know, if your research is on target, that he's up to his eyeballs in nefarious dealings with the towing-company racket, which the mayor is winking at with pleasure."

"Why 'with pleasure'?"

"By getting involved in a kickback scheme under the mayor's nose, Donnewald has handed Angelo Cira a personally engraved club that he can beat him with whenever Cira deems it advantageous. This could be one of those times. 'You rat me out, I rat you out.'"

"Fourth, Cira, as I know from personal experience, is not above murder when angered. And if your wife had cracked under the pressure or got cold feet or started feeling guilty and decided to come clean publicly, that would no doubt piss him off. The fact that he could be facing ruin and hard time might just be enough incentive for Cira to silence her permanently. And he would know how to do it clean as a whistle."

"You really think—"

"Wait, I'm not done. Fifth and finally, if I'm right about points one, two, three, and four, you're next."

Gabriel had finally gotten his attention. The professor brought his hands together as if in prayer and lifted them to pursed lips. Gabriel watched in silence as Stone sat there, unmoving for several moments. Finally, he looked up.

"I want to ask you a question and want your honest reply. Can you do that for me?"

Gabriel sipped from his glass then set it down. "What's the question?"

Stone took a deep breath. "If you can't play St. Christopher and carry me safely to the other shore, will you become my Angel of Death?"

- 24 -

Snow blanketed everything and kept falling in a relentless swirl of fat flakes. They called out for another bottle and sat drinking as if there was nothing better to do.

Stone, with his feet propped up on the bed, proposed a toast to his wife. "She deserved better."

"You're not *that* bad."

"Not what I meant. Better than ending this way … gunshot … and…."

"Ah, yeah."

"The early days were best, when we were both struggling. Such high hopes. Now I can't believe it's all over, that it ended this way, that I'll never … Sorry, I'm a bit maudlin."

"Sorry? Hell, you got every right to be more than a bit maudlin."

"Yeah, well, it's in the blood. My people have wakes and share drinks with the deceased. You ever read *Finnegan's Wake*? Me either. Tried. Couldn't, despite my Irish blood."

"'The name Stone sounds Jewish, but you're clearly Catholic through and through."

"English and Irish and Scots. My ancestors changed it from McSomething or O'Whatsit."

"I can see you're fascinated by family genealogy."

"A chump preoccupation. We all share ninety-nine point nine percent of our DNA and can all be traced back to a common ancestor in Africa two hundred thousand years ago."

"Soul brother!"

"Best to distinguish oneself not by ancestry but accomplishment. Based largely on opportunity. What we're all about—land of opportunity. Witness America's ingenuity and success, the dregs of Europe, refugees, discards, and descendants of slaves end up leading the world in most every goddamn category."

"Every damn category 'cept education to hear Professor Jonathan Stone tell it."

"Still … something worth drinking to. And we're gonna change that, right?"

Gabriel raised his shot glass an inch. "Sure."

Stone appraised him. "How'd you ever make lieutenant?"

Gabriel frowned. "What do mean how'd I make lieutenant? With talent and hard work, like the rest of your American dregs. What are you insinuating?"

"An obvious solution to all your problems sitting right before you and you don't recognize it."

"Finish your lecture, professor."

"Assuming Ellen was murdered, though not by Angelo Cira or his connections, you could win a gold star by apprehending the actual perpetrator, right?"

"Unlikely assumption."

"Answer the question."

"Possibly."

Stone spread his arms. "Here I am. I'm the one with the motive—betrayed husband—and the opportunity."

"She was shot in St. Louis, Missouri. You're in Quincy, Illinois."

"Only two-and-a-half hours by car. I could have driven down yesterday, met with her, argued, pulled the gun that I knew was in her purse, and shot her sometime before dawn. I'd still have enough time to drive back here and make seven-thirty Mass. You even have evidence of my intent. I wrote that it would be easier and more gratifying to kill her than divorce her."

"But you're forgetting one crucial thing, Stone."

"What's that?"

"You're a wuss without the balls to shoot a Muscovy duck, much less your lawfully wedded wife. That is, unless you're the world's best actor who's got a veteran cop completely buffaloed into thinking otherwise."

"I'm a lousy actor. My high school drama club never allowed me a speaking part. Too sincere. A failing in a society where everyone wears masks."

"Masks again. Which reminds me … in answer to your prior question."

"What prior question?"

"Some time back. A minor detail: whether I was St. Christopher or the Angel of Death."

"Oh, that."

"Yes."

"'Yes' what?"

"Yes, I was sent to kill you."

"And I thought your job was to enforce the law. Anyway, I know you're not serious."

"Not direct orders. Everyone'd be satisfied if you just went away peaceably and quietly."

"Unlike Ellen."

"That's what we'd prefer."

"Antecedent?"

"Huh?"

"For the pronoun 'we'."

"Me and you. You and I."

"I already told you 'not quietly.'"

"Screw you, Stone. Should be easy at this point. You're making it hard."

"Then throw the damn flash drives in the river. Throw me in the river. Don't worry about doing the right thing, do the easy thing, and see how easy it is to live with that."

Gabriel stood and moved to the window overlooking the street. Dusk. Still snowing—maybe a half-foot or more. All was silent. He remembered as a child how quiet it was on snowy mornings. He could tell, even before he ran to the window to look out at the street, that it had snowed and softened everything.

"Let's think about this. Let's say I was to help you—"

"I knew you would."

"Not saying I am. But if I did, I'd have to come out of this clean and you'd have to come out alive. So the first thing I'd have to know is whether your wife killed herself or had help pulling the trigger." Gabriel turned. "That might take some time, if I can do it at all. In the meantime I'd have to keep you on ice."

"Figuratively speaking, I trust."

"Figuratively speaking."

"Go on."

"I'm thinking. Thinking how to get what I want out of this."

"So much for altruism."

"To hell with altruism. So-called 'good' acts always make the actor feel good, but what about everyone else?"

"Saint Thomas Aquinas tells us to seek the common good as more desirable than the individual good."

"I'm figuring on getting both."

"And so much for principled action."

"I'm going rise above principle."

"This I've got to see."

"No, I mean it, Jonathan. I think I can pull this off and get you more than you bargained for."

"How so?"

"If I can figure some way to land the big fish, I'd come out smelling like a rose and you'd be right with St. Thomas."

"Mixed metaphor. And clichéd."

"But you need to trust me."

"Trust you how?"

"With your life."

"Which means?"

"I want to use you as bait."

Stone stared at him and finally nodded. "That's better: fishing, bait. Much better grammatically. But I still don't like the sound of it."

- 25 -

Mayor Angelo Cira lived on Westmoreland Place, a gated street near the northeast corner of Forest Park lined with venerable mansions built when St. Louis was still America's fourth-largest city behind New York, Chicago, and Philadelphia. His home sat just a mile or two down Kingshighway Boulevard from the Hill—formerly Dago Hill—where Cira grew up in a shotgun bungalow. Gabriel pulled his Dodge to the curb in front of the three-story Italianate structure.

In the front yard a snowman with stick arms and stocking cap sat in front of spotlights that illuminated the home's marble façade against the black night. An electric candle glowed in each window. Gabriel rang the doorbell.

Cira himself soon appeared dressed in a charcoal cardigan and carrying the *Wall Street Journal*. As they shook hands Cira's wife came from the living room to the right, where stood an enormous Christmas tree with white lights. She pressed her cheek to Gabriel's.

"It's been a long time, Marie."

"Too long. Years, Carlo. You're still handsome."

"And you haven't changed a bit." She was a plain woman, late forties, hair dyed black. "The kids—how old are they now?"

"Angela's graduating from Rosati-Kain this spring, Carlo's a freshman at Saint Louis U. High, and Katie just turned ten. She's at St. Roch's."

Gabriel voiced approval but thought Jonathan Stone might be interested to learn that the mayor—the ultimate overseer of the city's schools—entrusted his own children's education to the Archdiocese of St. Louis rather than the St. Louis Public Schools.

Marie retreated to the living room. Cira led Gabriel into the den on the left and slid closed two tall, polished pocket doors behind them. He indicated wingchairs on either side of the cold fireplace and went to a drink cart where he poured two snifters of brandy. Then he picked up a remote, clicked it, and the gas fireplace roared to life.

"Cigar?"

"Why not?'

Cira sat across from him as they lit up. He looked tired and pasty. Difficult days for the city and for the mayor. The street department had run out of salt, year-end crime stats showed that St. Louis had retaken its title of Murder Capital, U.S.A., from New Orleans; and he'd lost his press secretary, mistress, and money-launderer all in one swoop.

"I read your report, Carlo. Good police work."

"Can you put that in writing?"

Cira smiled then fixed him with a gaze. "You sure you got this resolved?"

"Pretty sure."

Cira blew out a cloud of smoke. "'Pretty sure'? We can't have any fuckups here."

Gabriel studied his cigar for a moment, and then looked

up at his old friend. "Stone's subdued now, in shock, what with losing his wife. Blaming himself for her suicide. Suicide being a mortal sin, he's got all that Catholic guilt weighing on him. Says he almost went to seminary instead of grad school and that Ellen would still be alive but for him turning away from God. It's taken all the venom out of him."

"Catholic guilt's good for something." Cira chuckled.

"Besides, he tells me something went wrong with his computer storage and he lost all the research he was doing. He was keeping it in some online cloud account. I had my tech guy verify it. On top of that, a lot of the snooping he was doing was likely illegal—hacking into city files and such. So we have that hammer if we need it. But I don't think we will."

Cira tilted back his snifter then puffed on his cigar. "Can you stick with him for a few days, at least till after the funeral?"

"No problem. He trusts me. We've developed a relationship. He really has no one else."

The mayor watched the flames dance against the dark stonework of the fireplace. "I still don't like it, Carlo. I'd like some closure here."

And there it was.

"I hear you, Ange. I'm with you a hundred percent on that. I'm looking out for you, but I got to look out for me, too. Better to solve this the easy way with no unnecessary exposure for either one of us."

"I see where you're coming from. Don't you worry about that. I'm going to take care of you. I owe you. We're still partners, just like the old days."

In other words, bend over and grab your ankles.

"You bet," Gabriel said.

Cira stood and they again shook hands.

When Gabriel got back to his car he paused to again study the house: the festive lights in the windows, the children's snowman in the yard, the luxurious trappings, the cozy life of the Cira family.

§

The next evening Stone and Gabriel sat sipping beer in Gabriel's apartment, not saying much, waiting. Gabriel had already filled him in on his latest meeting with Cira and what it might portend. Now Stone stared out the window toward the Arch while Gabriel studied his *English Grammar for Idiots*.

Even though he now had the English professor under wraps, he found he liked learning—or relearning—the rules of grammar. The English language was an intricate puzzle. Sentences were mysteries with subtle clues embedded in their structure, tone, and rhythm.

"Now they say it's okay to split infinitives."

Stone turned to him. "An anachronistic rule from fussy old grammarians. Splitting infinitives can help us to better express ourselves."

"Got it, professor."

Gabriel's cell phone buzzed. He answered, listened, and said, "Send her up, Carl."

He greeted Laura Berkman at the door. She went to Jonathan Stone as he rose from the sofa and took his hand.

"I'm so sorry about Ellen."

"She always respected you, Laura."

They sat and Berkman pulled a notebook computer from her leather purse and fired it up.

"I spent some time going over your research, Jonathan. Checked other sources and did some soft soundings of contacts in a very indirect way so as not to tip your hand. But I don't know if it's much of a hand right now."

Stone's shoulders sagged. Gabriel should have felt pleased, but found himself conflicted. Berkman went on.

"First, as to the ghosts in Treasurer Maurice Townsend's office. Yes, those folks are on the payroll and not earning their pay. But that's not so unusual in government these days. Cira's sister does have a degree in education and thus is not totally unqualified for a role as an educational consultant. And it doesn't come under the state nepotism rules as Cira didn't hire her—Townsend did.

"Townsend's pushing eighty and not running for re-election after thirty years, so there's little point in going after him. The other stuff—political hacks and union bosses on the payroll—standard operating procedure. We do a story on such shenanigans every few years. As a result a couple people disembark from the gravy train then get back on at the next station."

She glanced up at Gabriel and then continued. "The most obvious law-breaking here, Jonathan, is your hacking into the Treasurer's Office personnel files. And that's something Cira's people—which include prosecutors and judges—wouldn't be shy about coming after you for."

Stone stroked his beard. "I was in a state. Betrayed husband and all that."

She glanced again at Gabriel, who said, "We may get to

all that later, Laura."

"Okay," she said, "the campaign-contribution laundering is interesting, if we can prove it. Right now it's just hearsay you apparently culled from conversations with your wife."

"Not exactly hearsay," Stone objected. "Some of that info came from emails she sent."

"So you hacked into her computer as well?"

"Installed keystroke-monitor software. As I said, I wasn't myself."

"Anyway, only a prosecutor could verify this, and it would require subpoenas and such to access law firm files. I can dig into it but not sure how far I would get, maybe far enough to garner some official notice. But if you're out to get Cira, I doubt this would net him, only smaller fish."

"I'm not out to get anyone," said Stone. "I haven't even buried Ellen yet. But if not for this corruption, she might still be alive. My interest here is to do my duty."

Duty: a simple concept to some, such as Gabriel's father. But he saw that all three of them—Stone, Berkman, and himself—were bumping up against issues that were neither black nor white, as well as slippery political realities that made abstract moral concepts difficult to embrace.

"Sorry," said Berkman. "I understand." She returned her gaze to her computer screen and went on:

"Chief of Police Donnewald may be more vulnerable. Last year we did a story on his nephew leaving the scene of an accident in what had been an impounded vehicle, sold to him by Mound City Towing at a bargain-basement price. I checked with the reporter who covered that, and he's eager to follow-up if you can steer him to some hard data.

"Lastly, the Stadium Towne kickback scheme…"

"I know," said Stone. "Hearsay and illegally acquired data. Something that would take an interested prosecutor, subpoenas, et cetera, to prove."

"I'm afraid so. But I can start digging. Your wife's pass-through account is a good place to start. But I've no great hopes that it will lead anywhere. I'm sure Cira and his folks are covering their tracks as we speak."

Stone was nodding. "Okay, okay. I see." He looked to Gabriel. "But I have another card," he said, "that Carlo didn't reveal. A file he didn't include among those he sent you."

Gabriel lifted his chin at him. "You sure, Stone?"

"I'm certainly not worried about saving face at this point. And as far as Ellen's legacy is concerned—I want her death to serve a purpose."

Gabriel turned to Berkman. "We'd hoped this would be enough, Laura. What I didn't send you was Jonathan's documentation of Ellen Cantrell's affair with Cira. Much culled from her personal computer, which has now legally fallen into her husband's hands. And her admission of it to Jonathan, which he has on audio files."

"Not proud of that, either," Stone said, "surreptitiously recording conversations with my wife. But at least then it's not just hearsay."

Berkman shrugged. "But sexual escapades won't even bring down a president or a preacher these days unless it's with children, house pets, or farm animals. It might be a personal problem for the mayor, good family man that he is. And in March it might cost him votes with the church ladies—maybe enough for Alderman Milton Holmes to squeak past him in the primary, maybe not. But I don't see what purpose it would serve except to make my paper look like *The National Enquirer*."

Gabriel spread his hands. "But what about Cira's contribution to and complicity in her suicide, if that's what it was?"

"We don't know her mind. Her death could be totally unrelated to Cira."

"Come on, Laura. Mistress with the goods on a corrupt pol ends up shot to death. I'm a cop, you're a journalist. That doesn't raise any red flags for you?"

"'Mr. Mayor, a follow-up, please. Did you kill your press secretary?'"

"He's certainly nervous about something," said Gabriel.

"If Stone's right, Hizonor has a lot to hide."

"If *I'm* right that could include murder."

"But there's no indication of that," said Berkman.

"Because Cira's bum boy Donnewald has no doubt contaminated or destroyed all the physical evidence."

"Then bring in C.S.I. St. Louis. You might get a TV show out of it."

Gabriel glared at her. "You may know City Hall backbiting, Ms. Berkman, but you don't know shit about murder."

"You may know the street, Lieutenant Gabriel, but not legal nuances."

"Yes, this is much too subtle and legally nuanced for a dumb-ass cop noted for thumping defenseless prisoners."

"Not that again."

"I'll tell you one thing, Laura, this city was a hell of lot safer before you bleeding hearts got control of the police commission and courts."

"If we left it to you cops, we'd have watchtowers on every corner."

"That's right, we're all Gestapo at heart. But how about this? Cira told me point blank he wants *me* to make sure he gets 'closure' on this. What exactly do you think that means, Laura? What do you think he's asking me to do? Give Professor Stone a bitch slap?"

Stone stood and gazed out over the park while Gabriel and Berkman argued, taking no notice when they left. After Gabriel walked Berkman to her car, he returned to find Stone outside on the balcony, coatless, gripping its cold iron rail, staring east toward the apartment he shared with Ellen, the Arch, and the Mississippi.

Gabriel froze, then stepped across the room, eased open the balcony door, and moved behind him, ready to grab him if he made a move. Twenty floors below, traffic hummed past on the boulevard.

Gabriel whispered, "Jonathan…"

Stone nodded and without turning said, "Okay, Carlo. We'll do it your way."

- 26 -

The next day, a little before noon Stone and Gabriel stepped from his apartment and rode the elevator down. The cop led the former professor out the side door of his high-rise onto Rosebury Avenue.

"We'll walk. It's only a few blocks and there won't be any parking anyway."

Stone nodded.

The midday sky hung crisp, dry, calm, and cloudless. A beautiful day for a funeral. They walked down the middle of the plowed street, though many of the apartment-building sidewalks still held a half foot of snow.

"You okay?" Gabriel asked.

"Just."

"I'm sure it will be a media circus. You up to it?"

"Yeah, but is all this necessary?"

"You agreed to the plan."

"I mean the twenty-four-hour babysitting."

"I need to show Cira I'm best situated to control and deal with you. We don't want him sending anyone else to supply some 'closure.'"

"If you're trying to scare me, you're doing a good job."

"I'm scared, too, but don't want to rush in. I need to

solidify my position. Besides, we still don't know for sure if Ellen killed herself or whether Cira was somehow involved. If the latter, the stakes go even higher."

"Seem pretty freaking high already."

"Right you are, professor. Lots of potential downside if we fuck up. Not like teaching English, where the worst that can happen is to leave your participles dangling. We're balls out, my friend, both of us."

Gabriel was right about parking: Even two blocks away there was no curb space. On Clayton Road, TV trucks with their satellite dishes sat in front of the mortuary, a white stone building from which a hearse- and limousine-led cortege fed double-parked down Concordia Lane.

Once inside, Stone moved to the front of the chapel and bent to embrace a sixtyish couple—the Cantrells, apparently—who sat facing a closed maple casket next to a large flat-screen TV. Stone sat beside the father. Gabriel stood beyond the last row, back to the wall cop-like.

He spied Laura Berkman seated near the front on the far right. He looked around but did not see the mayor. After a few minutes, however, he appeared, Chief Donnewald at his side. They moved up the aisle and sat midway on the left, where chairs had been reserved. As they sat, the service began.

First came a video of Ellen Cantrell's life—childhood stills; tape of her as on-air newswoman in college and in St. Louis; more of her as City Hall mouthpiece. No Jonathan Stone to be seen except for a single wedding photo.

When the screen went blank, a middle-aged man who had been sitting next to Mrs. Cantrell rose and introduced himself as the pastor at the First Presbyterian Church of

Kirkwood, an old St. Louis suburb. As he went on about the Cantrell family and Ellen, Gabriel tuned him out, focusing instead on Stone. When at last the minister invited the audience to bow their heads in prayer, Stone turned. His eyes met those of Gabriel, who shifted his gaze to the left, toward the mayor and the chief. Stone turned back ahead.

As the service concluded, Stone moved first, brushing by his in-laws and striding down the center aisle to Cira and Donnewald. Gabriel moved against the flow toward them. He arrived as Cira, holding out his hand expecting Stone to shake it, was saying, "If there's anything I can do, Jonathan, just let me know."

"I think you've done enough already." Stone ignored the mayor's outstretched hand.

"You're rightfully upset. Give it time."

"Time? An interesting choice of words. I think you'll be the one doing time." He turned to Donnewald whose mask of sympathy had vanished. "You, too, if I have anything to say about it."

With that Stone strode away to the waiting limousine that would carry him graveside. Cira and Donnewald scowled at Gabriel.

"'Subdued,' Carlo?"

"I better stick with him," Gabriel said, moving to follow Stone.

Cira clutched Gabriel's elbow. "We need to talk. Soon."

Gabriel nodded and hurried down the aisle after Stone. He joined him inside the warm limo, which had been waiting, engine idling.

"How'd I do?" Stone asked.

Gabriel grimaced. "I think it worked, but I wanted more

determination and dementia, loose cannon personified. Instead you go all professorial, 'An interesting choice of words, that.'"

"I did not say, 'that.' Anyway, I told you I couldn't act. Besides, I was scared shitless. When Donnewald glared at me I thought I'd soil myself."

Gabriel nodded. "He's one tough son of a bitch. Better buy some diapers, my friend. It's only going to get worse."

§

The cortege moved west down Clayton Road. Stone sat mute staring out the window. Gabriel likewise remained silent. At Lindbergh Boulevard they turned south. After another ten minutes they were pulling into a snow-shrouded cemetery and soon stopped near a green tent erected over a freshly dug grave. As they emerged into the cold, Stone moved toward the tent. Gabriel slipped away.

He walked past the arriving cortege, where friends, family, co-workers, and likely some curious citizens seeking to rub elbows with the downtown media/political crowd rose from their automobiles buttoning coats and pulling on gloves.

He moved over the hilltop and down into a shallow valley where, stepping off the plowed lane into ankle-deep snow, he found a blue spruce—his mother's favorite—that he had planted some ten years earlier and not seen since. There with gloved hands he brushed snow from a marker for Theresa Sanchez Abregon de Gabriel and Samuel Joshua Gabriel—the final date yet to be added to the latter.

His mother would be near eighty now. Both his

mother and father were from a different era, people who remembered the Great Depression and World War II. Folks from simpler times who believed in black and white, right and wrong, no room for discussion.

He offered up a silent prayer:

Don't make them suffer, Lord. They're good folks, despite his tough hide. Show them forgiveness for their shortcomings and remember their goodness, and I'll try to do the same. Grant me some forgiveness as well. And some guidance. Most of all protect me. I'm going to need someone to cover my back. Amen.

Gabriel crossed himself, turned, and made his way back up the hill.

- 27 -

Gabriel stood in the large, carpeted anteroom outside Cira's office chatting with the mayor's driver, Monroe. Small talk about mutual acquaintances on the job, who was retiring, who was moving up, who was slipping up. Soon they fell into silence. So much they could say about the city, the gangs, the kids on the street. But what was the point? It was a job like most jobs. People in other professions sorted through ideas, data, or fresh fruit, retaining the good, disposing of the bad. The criminal justice system, for which cops were the point men, did it with people.

Soon the double doors to the mayor's office opened and Cira stepped through with homeless shelter impresario the Reverend Norris Pritchard and two corporate execs, judging by their tailored suits and bright demeanor. After bidding them goodbye and exchanging words with his secretary seated in the expansive outer office, Cira led Monroe and Gabriel down the marble staircase, through the lobby, and outside to his Lincoln waiting on the east side of the building. Once inside the car Cira said to Monroe: "M.A.C."

The Missouri Athletic Club—membership by referral only—was located some eight blocks northeast, a ten-story, hundred-year-old building that overlooked Eads Bridge and the Mississippi River. Gabriel had never been referred. Just as well. The YMCA he could afford, not this, with its gourmet restaurants, luxury guest rooms, and squash courts. Its barroom had won a rare exemption from new anti-smoking laws. It was often where deals went down downtown—if one was in the position to deal. And today, for once, Gabriel felt he was.

The locker-room attendant found shorts and a tee shirt that fit Gabriel. Shoes were a problem but he finally located some size twelves in the lost-and-found.

Gabriel joined Cira on the indoor track that circled the gymnasium—deserted at three in the afternoon—jogging by his side.

"You keep in good shape, buddy," the mayor said.

"If you like pears. Thirty pounds over my playing weight."

"Which was what—thirty years ago?"

"I've been trying the low-carb diet."

"I'm just trying to keep things where they are: some weights, a little jogging…"

"I hate jogging. Going up and down the court, fine. Not running around in circles."

"Sometimes it's necessary to circle back, Gabriel, to cover your tracks."

Gabriel looked at Cira, but that was all the mayor had to say on the subject for now.

Back at their lockers they wrapped towels around their waists and found an empty steam room. Cira pressed a button on the wall and steam began to billow from radiators. As he sat, Cira said, "Figured this was a good place for us to talk."

Gabriel grabbed his towel as if to discard it. "Want to do a cavity search?"

Cira laughed. "Can't be too careful. We need total confidentiality on this. Not even Donnewald needs to know."

"Know what?"

He fixed Gabriel with a stare. "How we're going to deal with Stone."

"I'm dealing with it."

"You're dealing with it? What the hell's going on? I thought you had him under control. What's he talking about yesterday? He doesn't have anything."

"Maybe he does."

"What do you mean?"

Gabriel sat. "I think he has backup files."

"You 'think'?"

The thick steam made Gabriel cough. "I've been playing 'good cop.' After he buried his wife, we had drinks and he spilled his guts. Claims he's hidden copies somewhere."

"Get them, whatever it takes."

"Believe me, I'm trying. I'm just saying it may not be easy."

"Get them. Even though he got half the stuff illegally, he could cause problems. And we don't need him stirring up shit about his wife's connection to me and her suicide. I need this election. It's closer than the wise guys think, and Holmes has something up his sleeve. My word from D.C. is that the president might come to do the ribbon cutting on Holmes' halfway-house project—that is, stab me in the back for being on the wrong side in *his* primary run. Fucker. Bottom line, Carlo, if I don't get this election then my

Stadium Towne deal—which the city needs—is finished, along with everything else I've worked for."

"I hear you."

"If Holmes got his hands on this stuff … Shit," Cira shook his head and looked away.

Gabriel took in a deep breath. "And something else, Ange. When he was schnockered, Stone alluded to something really explosive. I tried to pump him on it but he clammed up tight. I don't know what it is—photos, audio, documents. Could be anything. He's one of those computer geeks."

"That son of a bitch. With all this computer stuff around these days who knows who's got what anymore. Hard to do business. We got to stop him."

"Maybe some real-world education would do the trick."

"What are you talking about?"

The steam's hiss brought to mind the image of a serpent. Then the Garden of Eden. Forbidden fruit. Temptation. Knowledge.

"If he learned his wife didn't kill herself, it might give him pause, might make him step back, reconsider everything."

Cira studied him. He opened his mouth to speak, but Gabriel kept going.

"Don't bullshit me, Ange. If I'm going to do your dirty work, don't be blowing smoke up *my* ass. If I can persuade him that you or yours pulled the trigger, I think I can get him to cough up the backup files. Just look at him. The guy's a pussy. He'll he shitting his pants."

Cira covered his face with his palms and sat frozen, elbows on his knees as the steam swirled around him. "That's what you get when you fuck around with amateurs.

His wife was the same. As soon as she learned what he'd been up to, she panicked. Worried about her schmuck husband's whereabouts and welfare. Talking about going to the F.B.I. Dumb of her to tell me. Jesus H. Christ. Did she think I was going to let her go to the feds?

Gabriel swallowed. "I need a scenario, something to make him a believer."

The steam sputtered to a halt. Gabriel waited. His heart raced, blood thrummed in his ears. At last Cira spoke without looking up.

"Okay. Here's a plausible one. That night I spoke at the Martin Luther King dinner at the Chase. Afterward I called her from a phone at the hotel and told her we had to talk. I walked across the street into Forest Park where she picked me up. Had her park where there'd be little traffic. I knew she carried the Seecamp in her purse since she always had to lock it away when we traveled. Afterward I walked home. It took less than fifteen minutes. Good enough?"

"I can fill in the blanks."

"Tell him whatever works." Cira looked up. "Shouldn't be that hard. But once we've got the files, I don't want him having a change of heart. He might have backup files. We can't trust this guy. He thinks he's too smart."

"Meaning what?"

"He needs to vanish for good this time."

Though but a few feet distant, Cira appeared like an apparition through the steam.

"I hear you but—"

"I need you to come through for me, Carlo. Like you used to."

"There's risk."

"You're a smart cop. You know how to do things."

"Big risk deserves big reward."

"I said I'd take care of you."

"The price has just gone up."

Cira stared at him. After some seconds he said, "Name a figure."

"I was thinking seven figures."

"You're fucking me."

"I gauge that's just Ellen Cantrell's share. If I pull this off, the best place for me is south of the border. Early retirement. I've come to hate the goddamn winters. Summers suck too."

"I should assign you to the Tourist Bureau. Look, Carlo, I can't get that kind of cash together without leaving a trail a mile wide."

"I trust you for it, Ange. It doesn't have to come upfront or in a lump. I plan to have a long retirement. Just dribble it to me."

"All right. We'll figure something."

"And one other thing. We're partners again. We do it together. I don't want my ass hanging out to dry. No middlemen. Hand-in-hand so we have the omertà in full operation."

"You've already thought this through, haven't you?"

"I figured it was coming. You'd already said as much, so yeah, I'm looking out for me, Ange. But I'm looking out for you, too. I'm not going to let this little weasel take either one of us down. Besides, I'll be up to my neck in it myself."

Cira leaned across and put his hand on Gabriel's bare knee. "But it has to happen now, Carlo. Can't give Stone any time to figure out how to fuck us. We need to move fast. And it has to be clean. This all needs to be washed away quickly. Got it?"

Suddenly the steam kicked back on.

"Got it."

"Good. Set something up for tomorrow."

"Not much time."

"You know some places. This guy has to go back in the river."

- 28 -

After retrieving his car at City Hall, Gabriel picked up Stone at his condo on the east side of the park. Stone said he needed some fresh air so Gabriel drove to Art Hill and parked on its western ridge. Together they walked to the crest, toward the statue of St. Louis who sat his steed with sword drawn, arm held high as if blessing the city spread out before him. Rising temperatures and bright sunshine had shorn the slope of usable snow for sledders. A burnt-wood aroma from the cold bonfires hung in the air.

Gabriel stood back while Stone went to the low wall there and gazed out over the Grand Basin toward the apartment buildings that lined the park's northern edge, rose-colored at sunset.

"It really hit me today," Stone said. "Yesterday, when we went to my place to get my suit for the funeral, I was still numb. But this morning, I woke to her aroma in the sheets. The things she loved—art and cooking and, I don't know, simple things we'd shared over the years—were all around me and I just can't grasp that she found this world so lacking that she'd want to leave it forever."

Gabriel drew in a breath. "She didn't kill herself, Jonathan. Cira did."

Stone turned, studied Gabriel's face.

"You know for sure?"

Gabriel brought his gloved hands together. "Your disappearance likely triggered some anxiety and insecurity on her part. Then, after I revealed to her what you had unearthed, she apparently did some soul searching and acknowledged her duplicity and her responsibility for what she had done to you and to your marriage. She made up her mind to come clean and go to the feds with it, but made the mistake of telling Cira. He dissuaded her in the only way he could."

Stone ran his hand over his face then lifted his chin toward the Art Museum behind Gabriel. "I need to sit down."

They found a leather-covered bench in a gallery in the east wing.

"Degas," said Stone.

"Where?"

Stone indicated a painting to his left. "'Ballet Dancers in the Wings.'"

"Yeah, nice."

Stone took a breath and blew it out slowly. "I'm not going to start beating myself up again, but this news makes me feel even more guilty and stupid and selfish."

"I suspect it would. But it wasn't you who let yourself be corrupted and it wasn't you who pulled the trigger."

"So uncharacteristic, what I did to precipitate this."

"But it had the desired effect—to make her come to her senses and do the right thing."

Stone turned to Gabriel. "We need to do what she wanted to do, go to the F.B.I."

Gabriel pursed his lips. "I suppose we should. But with them things take time. Cira wants something to happen fast."

"Wants what to happen?"

"For you to vanish."

"I guess that doesn't mean another bus trip."

"No, it doesn't. A blow to the head and a dip in the river, so if they ever found you it'd look like suicide. I've agreed to arrange it, but with the caveat that Cira has to be in on it so he can't hold it over me."

Stone studied the Degas. "Admittedly I'm an amateur in these things, but given that my life's on the line I think I have the right to an opinion. We need to go to the feds."

Gabriel followed Stone's gaze to the painting. The ballerinas, exhausted, seemingly awaited their cue, looking like puppets whose strings have been slacked.

"Okay, okay. You're right. But I need to go to them with something other than just suppositions and a hard-on. A lot for them to swallow: the mayor a murderer, the police chief covering it up, multimillion-dollar kickbacks, corruption up and down the riverfront. A tall tale worthy of your Mark Twain."

"Without the humorous bits."

"Yeah. But it still may be a tough sell. Best to go in with a plan so they don't have to do much thinking, just provide tech support and backup."

"You have any ideas?"

"Let me think on it. Cira knows all the angles. He was a tough cop and a seasoned prosecutor, so he's seen it all. He'd smell anything fishy a mile off. We've got the cover for a plausible suicide, distraught young widower who has lost everything. The fact that you disappeared previously shows a precarious mental state and makes it even more convincing. But the setup can't have any strings showing.

"And I have to be careful for the double cross—though I think it unlikely. He trusts me and figures I'm a safe bet. Particularly as I'll be in Mexico with the million I get for killing you and sweeping all this under the rug."

Stone scratched his beard. "I think you made a mistake."

"What—I asked for too much money?"

"I believe you meant to use the conditional mood, '*I'd* be in Mexico with the million I *would* get for killing you,' a hypothetical state of affairs; not the future tense, '*I'll* be in Mexico with the million I *will* get,' which marks events expected to happen."

Gabriel nodded. "Right. My error."

- 29 -

Late next afternoon when Gabriel returned to his apartment, where he had Stone sequestered all day, the professor appeared drawn and shaky.

"You see the F.B.I.?" Stone asked.

Gabriel discarded his overcoat, went to the liquor cabinet in the kitchen, and poured himself some bourbon. Gabriel held up the bottle. "You?"

Stone shook his head.

Gabriel led him to the living room carrying the bottle and lowered himself onto the sofa. "Yeah, I saw the feds."

Stone stood over him. "What'd they say?"

"Said it's going to be tricky."

"How so?"

Gabriel felt himself anger and took some whiskey as suppressant. He had enough weighing on his mind without a bunch of questions from an English professor. But he needed him compliant, not skeptical.

"We have a meeting set for tonight."

"With the F.B.I.?"

"With Cira."

"What for?"

"This is the show. It goes down tonight."

Stone blanched. "Already? Where?"

"Won't know till I hear from the mayor himself. Why don't you sit down?"

Stone turned away and stared out at the dusky park, where the shadow of Gabriel's building lay across the snow as the sun set behind it. "I didn't realize they were that quick. They got you wired and everything?"

Gabriel took another drink. "Everything's taken care of. All you have to do is follow the script."

Stone turned back. "What script?"

"One the F.B.I. devised. We'll go over it a couple times before we leave. It'll be easy, even for a crappy actor like you. Now no more questions."

"Excuse me for being curious, but you've asked me to trust you with my life, and this sounds dangerous."

"Piece of cake. Just do what I tell you. Cira will be carrying, so you can't fuck up."

Stone swallowed. Gabriel poured himself another, hoping that he, Carlo Gabriel, was a good enough actor so Stone would not sense he was being deceived.

"You seem distracted, Carlo."

Gabriel again lifted his drink. "I'm thinking. Thinking how this will hasten my retirement so I can put all this shit behind me."

Stone stood looking at him wide-eyed, as if scared half to death. Just as well.

§

They went over the script a couple times, simple as it was. Stone had been right. He was no actor. But he didn't have to act much. His role called for him to play a terrified English professor.

It was almost seven o'clock when Cira called. "You know that second place you talked about? See you there in a half hour. Let's make it quick. I've got an eight o'clock town hall on the North Side."

"We'll be there."

Gabriel put the cell phone in his pocket and turned to Stone.

"We're on. Get your car keys. You're driving." Gabriel clipped his off-duty pistol, the Smith & Wesson seven-shot, to his belt and pulled on a shoulder holster containing his service pistol, a 92 D Beretta 9 millimeter semiautomatic. He slid the weapon from its holster and checked to make sure he had all fifteen rounds in the magazine and one in the chamber. When he turned, Stone was standing stock-still, staring at him.

Once outside and in Stone's Chevy, Gabriel directed him downtown on the interstate, then north on Broadway. Then, within minutes, onto Ferry Street toward the river and the massive, two-story high, concrete floodwall that lined it and protected the city when the Mississippi swelled. They moved through open metal gates.

"Left."

"That's the bike trail."

"Not tonight."

Trees cordoned the river, which flowed black but for slabs of gray ice dotting its surface. After a few hundred yards Gabriel spied a break in the tree line.

"Turn here."

Stone moved the old Chevy into a frozen-mud clearing

where sat a late-model SUV that had been stripped of its wheels and doors. Beer cans, plastic buckets, and other trash littered the plot. Dead ahead just yards away the dark river churned.

"Kill the engine."

"Scenic," said Stone.

"Turn off the lights."

"Now what?"

Gabriel took a breath. "We wait."

Stone stared ahead at the river. "You sure you know what you're doing?"

Gabriel turned to the professor and repressed an urge to slap him. He wished he had brought a flask.

"Stick to grammar, Stone, as you know fuck all about police work."

"Where's the F.B.I.?"

"If you could see them then Cira could certainly spot them."

"Wait a minute...." Stone turned to Gabriel. "How do they know where we are? After you got the call from Cira you didn't tell anyone the time and place."

Gabriel looked out the side window at the snow-covered earth.

"Where are the feds?"

"We don't need no stinking F.B.I. fucking up my deal."

"What are you saying, Carlo? Didn't you go to them?"

"Yeah, I went."

"And what?"

"I showed them the files and filled them in on everything. Their preliminary take mirrored Laura Berkman's. 'We need more evidence. This is going to take an investigation, subpoenas, et cetera.' They wanted to vet you to see how useful you'd be and then set up an elaborate sting to get Cira to cop to what he told me in the steam room, that he shot your wife and wants you dead, too. Then the other dominoes—the chief, the developers, the bankers—would fall."

"Why aren't we doing that?"

"Cira won't wait. And they wanted to run me and the whole operation and turn it into a Broadway production. They were going to get the credit for it and I'd get dick. Guys on the job wouldn't respect me ratting to the feds. There'd be nothing in it for me."

"What is it with you, Gabriel? You want to be chief of police?"

"No, Stone. Nothing to do with promotion or retirement package or anything like that. I want to do the right thing, like you said. But the right thing for me. Which means standing up to Cira and standing up for myself."

"Mother of God. You mean it's just you?"

"After I met with the F.B.I. this morning I got a call from Cira pressing me. If I tried to stall him to fit the feds' schedule he'd smell a rat. They don't know Ange like I do. I figured I better move. Just wing it solo and hand everyone a fait accompli."

"Wing it? What about the wire, the bug?"

"The Gecko's got it all fixed. I'm wired like a grand piano."

"I don't know, Carlo. This is making me nervous."

"You're making *me* nervous."

"It's so fucking dark and desolate here."

"Exactly. Now just shut up. I know what I'm doing. Trust me."

"I do, but I … maybe I shouldn't."

Gabriel turned and studied Stone's profile in the dim light. "You are right about that, Stone. You're a trusting bastard, and that trusting nature is a two-edged sword. Leaves you open to both good people and bad."

"I'll take my chances."

"As with your wife?"

"That's cruel, Carlo. Unworthy of you."

Gabriel sniffed. "You think I'm a good guy, on the side of God, on your side. But maybe you've miscalculated."

"You're spooking me, lieutenant. Stop it."

"You study the Apocrypha in religion class? Stories thought to be true but are misleading."

"Of course."

"So follow me. I once told you a story to help gain your trust. About how a pissed-off cop shot an unarmed suspect in cold blood and got his partner to cover for him."

"That didn't happen?"

"Oh, it happened all right. But I altered the plot a bit."

"I'm listening."

Gabriel took a breath. "It wasn't Angelo Cira who pulled the trigger, Stone. It was his partner. It was me."

"What?" Gabriel could hear Stone breathing hard.

"Me who compromised Cira and got him to cover my ass. I'm the one capable of cold-blooded murder, Stone. I'm the one who owes Angelo Cira a big favor, which I'm now going to square." Gabriel reached for his Beretta. "Get out of the car."

"You can't mean it!" Stone's eyes showed the realization taking hold, the rising panic. Voice cracking, he whispered: "You can't just kill me. I … I…"

Gabriel reached across and patted his knee. "See what a silly, trusting bastard you are, Stone? Nah, I'm not going to kill you," he said re-holstering his Beretta. "I just made all that up to show you you're way out of your league."

Stone sat glaring at Gabriel. "You vicious son of a bitch."

Gabriel laughed. "That's the way we roll. When it comes to vicious, you backstabbing English teachers got nothing on the S.L.P.D. The old adrenaline's going now, eh?"

"Liked to stop my goddamn heart, you bastard. If we get through this alive I'm going to kill you with my bare hands."

"Judas. But at least you're finally manning-up."

Headlights swept across the riverbank in front of them and dimmed. A Buick SUV pulled beside them.

"Don't lose that adrenaline rush, Stone," Gabriel muttered. "And follow the goddamn script."

They rose from the Chevy and moved toward the Buick. As they did, its door opened and Angelo Cira stepped out in a black overcoat. Stone stopped in his tracks and turned to Gabriel.

"What's he doing here? What's going on?"

The mayor approached and stood beside Gabriel. "Your man sounds surprised, Carlo."

Gabriel smelled the dark Mississippi rushing by, the scent of earth brought from the plains by the Missouri, which joined it scant miles upstream. "He was expecting the F.B.I."

"The F.B.I.'s downtown, Stone. You made a wrong turn."

Stone closed his eyes and lowered his chin as if praying. Then he looked up to Gabriel. "You never went to them?"

"Nope. Spent a relaxing day playing hoops and meditating in the sauna."

"I trusted you with my life."

"We gave you a way out. You decided not to take it."

Cira said, "You got the files, Carlo?"

Gabriel reached into his coat pocket and withdrew two flash drives. "Right here. They can go in the river with the professor."

Stone turned on Cira. "I guess you gave Ellen the same chance before you killed her."

Cira looked at Stone then shifted his eyes to Gabriel. "Come on, let's get this over with. Fucking amateurs, both of them, him and his sweet-assed wife."

Cira strode toward the river. Gabriel, heart pounding in his throat, reached for Stone. Stone tore lose from his grasp and rushed Cira from behind.

"What the hell!" called Gabriel.

Cira turned at the sound. Stone reached him and threw a wild right that caught the mayor behind the ear. The two went to the ground hard, wrestling on the snow-covered earth. Cira quickly threw him off and rose drawing a pistol from his coat pocket.

"You motherfucker!"

Gabriel dashed forward to lay a hand on Cira's arm. "Don't, Ange! We need him in one piece. This needs to look like a suicide, not an execution."

"Then club the bastard and dump him in the goddamn river."

"Okay. Just put the gun away and give me a rock. This has to look right in case they find him."

Gabriel pulled Stone from the ground and marched him toward the river. Cira awaited them on the bank, grasping a rock from the riprap there.

"Go ahead and do him if you want, Ange."

"With pleasure."

Gabriel's cell phone binged. With his left hand he lifted it from his coat pocket and read a text message from The Gecko: "Got it!"

He turned to Cira. "No, let me do it. You don't want any blood on you for your meeting."

Cira handed him the rock.

"Now," said Gabriel, "hand me your gun, Ange."

Cira turned to him slack-jawed and focused on Gabriel's Beretta, now trained on him. "What the fuck?"

"Sorry, Ange. This is where our one-sided relationship ends. Angelo Cira, you are under arrest for all kinds of nefarious shit: murder, racketeering, corruption, et cetera, et cetera. I'll read you your rights, all recorded, so there's no Miranda bullshit in court."

"You fuck! You won't pull this off, Gabriel. You're nobody."

"I'm going to try. Give me your gun."

"Fuck you. I'm leaving. I have a meeting. I don't think you'll shoot me in the back. Wouldn't look good to assassinate the mayor."

Cira turned and moved toward his SUV twenty yards distant.

Gabriel licked dry lips, watching, mind racing. When the mayor reached the vehicle and grabbed the door handle Gabriel raised his pistol, aimed, and fired, the explosion echoing off the floodwall and ringing across the river.

Cira pressed himself to the car then turned to see the shredded front tire. Gabriel aimed next at the rear tire and squeezed off a second round. Cira started. Then he turned, pistol in hand. Gabriel aimed a third time.

"Put the gun on the ground, Ange, or I start with your kneecaps."

§

Once he had Cira handcuffed and in the back seat of Stone's Chevy, Gabriel called his FBI contact and asked for a ride. It took a couple minutes to convince him it wasn't a prank and he was mostly sober.

He and Stone awaited the feds' arrival, standing off to the side in the trees, Gabriel alert to whatever might be coming down the bike trail. He doubted that Cira had involved Donnewald or private backup—i.e., mobsters or gangstas—in tonight's meet. But he had come too far at too much risk to get lax now.

"You went off script, Stone. Big time. What the hell got into you? A fricking English teacher jumping an armed ex-cop."

"I told you I wasn't much of an actor. But I do have an imagination. Looking at Cira I saw him and Ellen in bed together. Then I pictured him putting the gun to her head, heard her pleading for her life. And the dismissive way he treated me … I just snapped."

Gabriel kept scanning the dark scene before him as the river roiled behind him. "If you jump everyone who's dismissive you'll grow a hell of a rap sheet."

"Anyway, it worked. Got him pissed-off enough to drop his guard and want to kill me, too." Stone's breath came in short bursts, white vapor clouds hanging in the icy night. "Never thought I'd like police work. It's not so bad."

Gabriel glanced at Stone then returned his gaze to the darkness before him.

"You're still on the adrenaline high, Stone. And tonight's not normal … But no, it's not so bad, not if you're doing it right. We're all on the same side—coppers, teachers, snowplow drivers, judges, and politicians. Or should be. And maybe you were right after all, we all need to do the right thing to make it work."

The harsh searchlight from a towboat moving upriver flashed by the shore and laid a bright silver band across the black Mississippi.

"Where do you think this will land you?" asked Stone.

Gabriel again became conscious of the river's fertile aroma and the sound of its rush. "God knows. Could end up as chief of police or in the big house. More likely somewhere in between. But wherever, I'll land on my feet. Always have. I suspect you will too once you sort through all this."

Stone nodded. "Neither one of us is up the river or the creek yet."

Soon headlights—two pair—appeared coming north up the bike trail and stopped before the turnoff to the treeless area where Stone's Chevy and Cira's shot-up Buick sat.

Gabriel stood with a gun in both hands, watching, praying.

- 30 -

Carlo Gabriel sat at the umbrellaed café table in slacks, loafers, and guayabera, studying the lunch menu and sipping a lemonade. Its scent and a warm westerly breeze wafting down the street from Forest Park made him think of hot childhood days and trips to the zoo.

He glanced up to see Stone—now clean-shaven and wearing cargo shorts, tee shirt, and sandals—coming down the sidewalk on Laclede Avenue from his apartment building, looking like a college kid. They shook hands.

Stone sat across from him and said: "You seem relaxed."

Gabriel studied a chirping sparrow in a nearby gingko tree shading them. "Feeling very chill these days despite the heat."

"What's changed?"

Gabriel held his arms out to his sides. "Notice anything different? Perhaps my new streamlined look."

"Lost weight?"

"A pound and a half: my pistol."

"You get busted?"

Gabriel laughed. "Not that they didn't try, for all the irregular crap I pulled. No, I turned fifty-five last week and took retirement. Funny, after carrying a gun for thirty years,

I feel naked."

"What prompted this?"

The waitress came and Stone ordered iced tea. When she'd gone, Gabriel said,

"There was nothing more to prove."

"What about promotion and getting back in the loop at headquarters?"

"You've been following Laura's stories, I guess. You see how the legal stuff's dragging on. Looks like Cira could take a walk on Ellen's murder. He's fighting admissibility of the audio files from the night we took him down. All they may have left is me versus the mayor, he said, she said, so to speak. And the other stuff—the corruption, the conspiracy to commit murder, et cetera—will take years to prepare and adjudicate. Meanwhile I'd be in limbo."

"At least he and Donnewald are gone."

"Not sure Holmes and Coleman are a marked improvement. Same for the new treasurer. They're covering the tracks on everything you exposed. And it looks like the Stadium Towne deal will go ahead, though with a different starting lineup. Everyone wants it: the team, the fans, the developers, downtown businesses, the bankers. Hell, I'll probably go enjoy a few brews there."

"Who said you can't fight city hall."

"You can fight it, but it fights back. And I'm tired of struggling. I've got better things to do and enough money to do it."

"Like what?"

"Been brushing up on my Spanish, which I haven't used since my mom died. I've got cousins in Jalisco whom I haven't seen in years. I'll start there. Then likely some fishing village far away from the *narcotraficantes*. Maybe I'll write a memoir, minding my misplaced modifiers. Or maybe I'll just try to forget it all. Speaking of writing, how goes your work?"

"Finished and submitted my dissertation just because I don't like loose ends. Working my ass off at the charter school, focused on the real world, the here and now. Nice to see tangible results, helping kids who need it and want it."

"So it's all good?"

The waitress reappeared with Stone's tea and he sipped.

"Ellen still haunts me, but I've forgiven her. Still trying to forgive myself. If I hadn't acted like a schoolboy, she'd still be alive."

Gabriel recalled the snowy day in Quincy, where he told him his wife was dead, and Stone, crushed and guilt-ridden, racing away as if to throw himself into the Mississippi.

"I don't know about that, Jonathan. Sooner or later you would have confronted her with your knowledge of her involvement in Cira's schemes, and you both might have ended up dead. You believe in God and providence and whatnot, right? Why not believe He had a hand in this?"

Now Stone studied the sparrow, pursing his lips. "I also believe in free will and being accountable for our acts."

Gabriel leaned forward. "Look, Stone. Let's make a deal. Flawed human being that you are, you start cutting yourself a little slack and stop trying to be the Son of God, himself, and me, created in His image, will start acting a little more like Him. Deal?"

Stone smiled. "Agreed. But I have another deal for you. You remember Alonzo Watkins, the chess player who got shot? He's okay now, physically, at least."

"But not otherwise?"

"He's bailing out, fixing to join the Army. I can't blame him. You know why he got shot?"

"I've found that people don't need good reasons."

"For acting 'white.' For carrying a book bag and a chessboard. For standing his ground when he probably shouldn't have."

"So he knew who shot him."

"Seems so. But he's understandably tight-lipped."

"Maybe a gang thing, an initiation. Wrong place, wrong time. Who knows?"

"I suspect he'll do all right in the service. But I'm also worried about the punks who attacked him and other kids who turn bad—not to mention their victims."

Gabriel nodded. "I've seen it ruin schools and neighborhoods. Just a few assholes terrorizing, intimidating, and undermining a community. Some of these kids are just irreversibly screwed up, kicked around, abused, abandoned, left to run wild. By the time we get our hands on them, it's too late."

"But it's not too late for my students," said Stone. "They come to the charter school hungry to grab something of life. But poverty's the thing that holds them back—not financial poverty, but a poverty of ideas and morals and a sense of responsibility for their own lives. The things parents and families are supposed to provide. It shackles them."

"I'm not optimistic you can set them free."

"But we have to try."

"Challenging work, Stone. Exactly what you were looking for."

"But I've bitten off more than I can chew. Luckily I work

with some good people who are trying to give the kids what their families and neighborhoods aren't."

"Good luck."

"Not as easy as teaching grammar. We've got social workers and psychiatrists and preachers helping us, but when the day is done most of the kids still have to go back to dicey neighborhoods."

"Any success?"

"These kids can do it if they work, but it's tough. Too many smart ones drop out, too many capable ones don't go to college."

Gabriel sipped his lemonade. "You said you had a deal. What does this have to do with me?"

"Here's the bottom line. Part of the problem with the guys is that they lack role models. A lot don't have fathers they know or trust. They need to figure how to deal with all the seductions and dangers on the streets—gangs, drugs, status issues, confrontations. They need to know things you know."

"I see where there is leading, but I'm not following."

"Come work with us, Carlo."

"Screw you, Stone. I'm going to Mexico."

"Mexico will always be there. You don't have to do this year-round or five days a week. No commitment. Just lend us a hand. You told me you lectured in schools and worked juvenile crime. You have insights that none of us teachers have."

Gabriel looked away. "You're asking a lot, my friend. Too many señoritas waiting."

Stone smiled. "At least come visit. No obligation."

Gabriel looked at him askance. "I always said you were a

sly mother. I come and have all these desperate kids hanging on me like I'm their daddy, kids I can't say 'no' to. Forget it."

"Think about it, lieutenant. What else are you going to do with your life now that you've gotten it back?"

"Gotten it back, my ass. I never lost it. Leave me alone with your moralizing, professor."

"No more 'professor.' I'm just a teacher trying to do his job."

"Fine for you. But I've done my job and done it for thirty years. I need some time away from all this."

"Which means you'll be back. That'll do for now."

Gabriel studied him. "You think you would have learned something through all this, Stone. Perhaps to be a little more pessimistic about people."

"It's your fault, Lieutenant Gabriel. I trusted you with my life. And here I sit, my faith in mankind restored."

Gabriel shrugged. But his was too.

Acknowledgements

My sincere thanks go to those who contributed to this book. First, four colleagues and fellow writers: John Leslie, who, upon hearing my tale of once trying to teach remedial grammar to inner-city junior-college students, planted the seed that led to this novel; Kelly R. Daniels, for his close reading of the early manuscript and substantive suggestions for improvement; Terry Baker Mulligan, who gave critical feedback on literary, educational, and African American issues; and Jayne Navarre, who provided insight into military family life and whose multiple readings and suggestions helped shape the book and its characters. Thanks also to rapper Cuda Brown for his help with contemporary urban English, to Joe Koerner for aid with things Jesuitical, and to editor Kristina Blank Makansi for her deft work on the manuscript.

Further, Lieutenant Mike Muxo, Director of the St. Louis Police Academy, provided much needed background on St. Louis Metropolitan Police Department organization, procedures, and equipment; Baxter Leisure, Executive Assistant at the City of St. Louis Medical Examiner's Office, gave me details about the city morgue, its operation, and its ambiance; and Cathy Heimberger, Director of Marketing for the Saint Louis Public Library, supplied information about the Central Library's recent restoration.

Any factual mistakes are mine.

About the Author

Former journalist Rick Skwiot is the author of three previous novels—the Hemingway First Novel Award winner *Death in Mexico*, the Willa Cather Fiction Prize finalist *Sleeping With Pancho Villa*, and *Key West Story*—as well as two memoirs: the critically-acclaimed *Christmas at Long Lake: A Childhood Memory* and *San Miguel de Allende, Mexico: Memoir of a Sensual Quest for Spiritual Healing*. He also works as a feature writer, book doctor, and editor. From St. Louis, he currently resides in Key West.

CPSIA information can be obtained at www.ICGtesting.com
Printed in the USA
LVOW11s1203101214

418145LV00001B/1/P